THE ROMANOV SISTERS

SVETLANA IVANOVA

CHAPTER 1

The apocalypse did happen.

But it wasn't the end of the world. It was the start of a tyrant world ruled by a superior race—the bloodsucking kind.

I had been running away from this nightmare-come-true for four years. Our family hid underground from the global chaos that went around the continents. The global domination was led by the newcomers.

In fact, the newcomers were not new but rather ancient. We remembered learning in school that Homo sapiens were not the only species to walk the earth, and we were right.

There were the Other Ones living among us.

Almost every culture has a mention of these beings. Since the ancient Mesopotamia, Greece, China, and India, there were accounts of bloodthirsty creatures recorded. They called this species 'vampires'. But before people accepted that they truly existed, it was already too late.

A hellish war began every night for decades. At first, humans were found dead in a dark alley or forest. Then people began to die with blood drained out of their bodies, shriveled and cold in the streets and in their homes then all over in the world. When the casualties increased and alarmed the governments, it had reached the rate of hundreds overnight before reaching thousands and millions.

The war came at us like nightfall but raged quickly like a hurricane. By the time, we knew what was going on; the Other Ones had built a stronger army to overthrow the human race. Everyone knew the future of humanity was doomed.

The Other Ones won the global war and raided every house and seized all that belonged to us. But that wasn't the worst part. The worst part came when the humans got enslaved throughout the planet. We became their property and even their sexual objects.

It was like those old Holocaust movies that we used to watch in school. Black-coated soldiers would kick the front doors of our houses and slaughtered both our young and old. They only kept the healthy ones. They needed blood supply for their New People.

I was fifteen when my family went into hiding. We'd been living an Anne Frank life for the last two years. My younger brother died because there was no medical treatment where we lived. Our shelter was among the hundred others along the abandoned railroads. Some of the people lost faith and agreed to serve the New People. They became the working class. If they were good with their servitude, their masters would give them a new life by turning them.

But there were others who avoided being captured— others like us.

However, the new kind would still hunt us down.

One day, we were found. I remembered that cold night after my brother died, a group of black soldiers burst into our humble refuge. They grabbed my father and pinned him against the wall with a blade. My mother screamed and screamed. I didn't know what to do. My knees dropped to the floor beside her. We shivered in fear. They then killed my father and then drained my mother out of blood right before my eyes.

But they took me with them.

The vampires handcuffed me and shoved me into the back of a black military truck. There were a dozen of girls and boys my age who were also captured that night. I still recalled the frightened look on their pale faces.

There was no telling where the Other Ones would take us. After a long ride in silence, we ended up in a huge white building, which looked like a hospital or some kind of science institution.

There they examined us in a large sterilized lab. Two women ripped off my clothes and told me to turn around. Their eyes shone in crimson color as they stared at my naked body. The humans who got turned always had faint rings of red around their pupils. They worked for the New Government.

There were three classes of them. The working class: red-eyed. The middle-class: violet-eyed. Then there was the high-class — the strongest of them all: eyes of rare vivid gold.

The golden-eyed vampires were resurrected. They came from the long-lost royal families around the world. Some of the royal families had been vanished for hundreds of years.

They suddenly came back to life and reclaimed what they lost.

No one suspected that the vampire race had been ruling the earth since the old day. They disguised themselves as royalties who received the authority from the higher power. The Ottoman Dynasty, the Shang Dynasty, the Hohenzollern Dynasty, and the Aryans, and other long-lost royal families around the world were now the New Orders. They resurrected from the Land of the Dead and reclaimed their lost empires. Those people didn't die. They had been hiding in the dark for hundreds of years. At last, they reunited and invaded our planet to create a new world.

But that was another long horrible bedtime story.

My life was predestined to a doomed fate by then. For five days, I got locked up with a bunch of sad-looking girls. They were waiting for two different fates just like me.

Wealthy vampires would buy humans for their fresh blood. Of course, the blood from the livings was warmer and more delicious than the blood bags. Or we would end up in one of their cruel factories where they pumped blood out of our veins and packed it and shipped it off for sale. It was like the way we used to do to cows and pigs at the butcher farms. Now it was our turn to endure this misery.

Then my fate changed. On the twentieth day, I was sold to an old royal house. One of the most powerful royal families bought me. That was how I met my mistress.

She was a Romanov.

CHAPTER 2

I found myself sitting in a black SUV the next day. There were two men in black suits sitting at the front. They wore sunglasses and had com units in their ears. Several other black cars drove ahead of us. After a while, I saw a glimpse of an iron gate appeared from the distance. The stone walls stretched far into the dark green forest surrounding the area.

The automatic gate opened. We drove through a massive courtyard with manicured gardens and overgrown oak trees. The smell of flowers seeped through the tinted window of the car. We kept crawling on the pebbled pavement that snaked toward an enormous mansion.

The building looked like the mansions in Florence. Those colossal sculpted pillars, statues, and marble fountains could be seen from afar. When the cars stopped, the door at my seat slid open.

"Get out," a man dressed in complete black said to me. I gingerly stepped out of the SUV with a pounding heart.

Then I realized there wasn't just me there. Five other girls and three boys were also brought along into this seeming paradise, or in our case — hell.

Before we left the Human Institution, they had made sure that we were well-groomed and well-fed. They spent a good part of our stay training us to be willing servants. I'd also got my skin scrubbed, my hair done, my nail polished, and body hair removed. It was a strenuous process on my part since I hated every minute of it.

Looking at the rest of us, I could tell the same thing happened to them. They looked perfectly healthy with glowing skin and beautiful faces, but as we stared at each other, I could see the nervousness in their eyes.

About ten guards came out of the grand double doors of the mansion and ushered us inside.

The main hall was even bigger than an average church's. Heavy thick scarlet draperies hung over the windows from floor to ceiling. Expensive furniture decorated the whole place. Ceramic vases and classic paintings lined up the walls.

"Wait here, humans," one of the red-eyed guards said to us. Others flashed their venomous teeth in a warning. We kept ourselves still and silent as they watched.

A moment later, another group of men walked into the hall. One of them wore a white suit with a brim of red around the collar. A red handkerchief popped out of his breast pocket. He had a tall and lean figure, shiny black hair, and violet eyes. The guards bowed at him as he walked past.

"Report," the man said in a deep voice. One of the guards hurried forward and handed him a clipboard. The man took it and examined whatever written on the papers.

"So they all have O positive blood?"

I'd heard that people with O blood had become so rare and expensive. For some reason I didn't know, the high-class vampires preferred the taste of it.

"Yes, sir." The guard nodded "But one of them is special."

"Who?" the man asked.

"That girl, sir," the guard pointed at me. The man looked up from the clipboard. My body shivered under his gaze.

"What's her blood type?"

"Hers is Rh negative, sir," the guard responded. "The rarest of her kind."

This piece of information shocked me. I'd heard that humans with this type of blood were already extinct under the vampire oppression. It was like finding a gem among the regular rocks.

"Wonderful," the white-suited man said and then walked forward. I froze in place as he circled around me with his piercing violet stare.

"What's your name?"

I couldn't find my voice to speak. The panic lump clogged my throat.

"Answer him, slave!" the guard hissed. I recoiled.

"My...my name is Av...Avery Pierce," I stuttered.

"You do smell different, too." The man nodded to himself. Then he turned to the others vampires. "Keep this one. Bring the rest to the servant house."

The guards started to move the others away.

The man walked up to me and cupped my chin in his cold hand. His violet eyes bore into mine.

"Be good and serve well, human girl," he said. "If you wish to stay alive longer, don't upset your mistress."

I grimaced. Then the man let me go.

"Now come with me," he said and turned to walk.

As the guards escorted me through the hallway, I looked around the place. We went up the main staircase. The mansion was massive. It might as well be a palace. I might have to spend a whole day just to find the nearest restroom.

We walked along the quiet archway. My high heels scrapped on the carpeted floor. We reached another majestic wooden door. The guards pushed it open. The groaning sound of wood sent a shiver down my spine.

But no one crossed the threshold as if there were some forbidden boundaries there. The man in the suit turned to me again and smiled.

"I hope you come back alive."

Then the guards shoved me into the room and locked the door behind me.

CHAPTER 3

I looked around the enormous chamber. It was too dark and too cold. I felt as if I had just stepped into a mountain cave. All the windows were closed. There was no one in sight. I tried the door again, but it was firmly locked.

I looked around the chamber.

The crested furniture lay around the sitting area. Another room led to a separate hall. I could see massive bookshelves from floor to ceiling and an elegant black piano by the balcony.

I decided to walk a few steps further into the room. Then I thought I heard a sound as I waited for something to happen. It was like a whistle of the wind.

At my right was the bedroom. The door was slightly ajar, revealing a canopied bed. There were sheer hanging and heavy silk curtains hanging from the four posts.

I had been living in a wretched place for too long that the sight of this elegant place lured me in. My feet drifted towards the beautiful bed without realizing it.

But then someone grabbed me by my hair and hurled me like a rag doll. I fell on the soft mattress.

"You like this bed, human girl?" a woman's voice spoke. I gasped and tried to get up, but a strong hand pressed me down by the throat.

I couldn't breathe, let alone speak.

I looked up to see a young woman atop me. Her long raven hair brushed over her shoulders like flowing black silk. She had bright golden eyes that burned hot like two miniature suns. They were mesmerizing to the mind of a prey, and I couldn't take my eyes off the strange woman.

Even in this horrible state, her face struck me speechless with its rare beauty. I had never seen a face like this. She was also heavier than she looked. I felt as if I was pressed by a hundred pound of flour sag. Maybe it was because of that immense strength that was hidden within her.

I began to choke. My hands tried to pry her hand off, but it was pointless. She was a vampire, too strong for my feeble effort to fight back.

Then the pressure subsided. The dark-haired woman let go of my throat yet still locked my body under her weight. I coughed violently.

"Now, speak." She raised her perfect eyebrows. Her face was inches from mine. I could feel her cold breath fanning my cheeks. She smelled like sweet-scented wildflowers in the deep dark forest. I expected the foul rotten odor for something that had been dead for so long, but not this.

"I...I..." I started but no words came out. Then I found myself sobbing.

"Shhh..." the woman coaxed at me. "You know why you're here?"

"Go ahead and kill me," I said at last.

She laughed.

"Oh in due time, but I'm not going to kill you now. I'm going eat you slowly and eat you well."

She gave me a wicked look. Her golden irises flickered like fire. Then she bared her teeth. My eyes widened as two flashing white fangs drew out of her gum like a cat's claws. They were as sharp as butcher knives. A frightened gasp escaped my lips. My heart began to beat against my ribs wildly. I tried to push her off me but she gripped my hands and clasped them over my head.

"Quite feisty this one," she said. "Are you a virgin?"

I didn't know what to say to that. But she nodded as if she already understood.

"Well, you're not going to be one for long."

Afterward, she held one of my wrists up and bit hard into it. I screamed in sheer pain. It was agonizing how her razor-sharp teeth sinking deep into my veins. Red blood dripped onto the silk cover.

Then the woman released my hand again.

"Damn, what a taste," she said as she licked her lips in satisfaction. "Too bad, I'm not hungry enough to devour you now. But this shall mark you as mine."

Just like that, she got off me and stood up by the bed.

"Now you can go." She gestured to the door. "But from now on, you're my special dessert, remember that."

I struggled to crawl out of her soft bed. A wave of dizzy hit me at the sight of my own blood. It stained like red roses on the white sheet. I managed to stagger to my feet again and stumbled out of the room.

The woman watched me go with an amused smirk on her face. She looked like she was in the early twenties, but I could never be sure what a vampire's real age was. Even so, she was the most beautiful woman I'd ever seen. And for a second there, I almost thought she couldn't be so evil.

I held my throbbing hand and slipped through the door then out of the dark cold chamber.

_*_

On the way through the hall, I turned the corner and bumped into someone. When I looked up, I saw another pair of beautiful golden eyes staring at me. I gasped, stumbling away in fright. But an arm wrapped around me by the waist and steadied me back. I realized I had stumbled upon another fanged-nightmare.

It was a young blonde woman.

"Are you alright?" her musical voice spoke with a hint of a Russian accent to me. I did not expect this kind of question.

"I'm...I'm fine, please don't hurt me," I murmured back in fear. The woman looked down at my blood-smeared hand. Her perfectly arched brows raised and her lips pressed into a thin line.

"It's my sister again, isn't it?" she said more to herself. Her liquid golden eyes stirred with emotions.

"I'm just a slave, what right do I have?" I said with a mix of anger and hatred. I couldn't help it. She could kill me for that if she wished. But the woman's smooth pale face marred with concerns. I didn't understand why.

When I started to walk away, she stopped me.

"I'll get you to your room," she said. "You look bad. She must've forgotten to turn off her venom."

"What?"

Before I could say anything else, she came to wrap her arm around my waist and placed my good arm over her shoulders.

I was shocked.

"What are you doing?" I cried. My face screwed in confusion.

"Stop talking or you'll pass out," she told me.

And she was right.

I felt my knees give way and my vision went blurry. Then I didn't remember anything else until I found myself in another bedroom. The place was plain and much smaller, but at least, it was brightly lit with opened windows. It must be the servant room.

My cut wrist was neatly bandaged. I looked around myself and saw the same woman beside my bed. Her long cascading blonde hair flirted with the breeze.

"Why are you doing this?" I whispered. "You're a vampire, aren't you?"

The blonde smiled at me. Her smile just took my breath away. It wasn't the cold wicked one I was used to, and it was beautiful.

"Just because I'm one doesn't mean I can't do this." She gestured to my bandaged hand.

"What's your name then?" I blurt. I was probably the first person who dared ask for a vampire's name.

"Anastasia," the young woman replied.

"Anastasia—?" I echoed her.

"Romanov," she added. "Anastasia Romanov."

It made me gasp in realization.

"The Russian royalty?" I said. I'd heard of that name before—it was mentioned in the history book that we used to study. "But—but didn't the Czar family all die at the shooting squad during the Russian Revolution?"

I couldn't help asking.

Surprisingly, Anastasia laughed. Her voice carried spring and summer music in it. I felt a little embarrassed for liking that sweet tone.

"I'm not going to argue with you about that," she simply said.

I kept staring at her face. She brushed a strand of her blonde lock behind her ear and looked away from my gaze.

"I'm sorry about my sister by the way," she said after a while. "Stay away from her and you'll be fine."

Now I could see the family resemblance when she mentioned the other woman. But I noticed Anastasia's eyes were softer and deeper like molten gold shining from the depth.

But I wouldn't bring myself to trust these dangerous creatures.

I hated them all.

"Why does it matter to you? Go away, I don't want your help," I said in bitterness and turned my back to her.

"Well..." Anastasia said with a low sigh. "I'll let you rest now."

Then she left the room without a sound.

CHAPTER 4

ANASTASIA

*I*t was maddening.

Something about the rattling sound inside her veins, the intoxicating smell of her skin, I couldn't stand one minute without wishing to taste her warm blood. And that's what I hated about myself. My predator instinct was unforgiving. Who was this girl?—an innocent human with a deadly charm? I held my breath the whole time I was near her. All details of her features stuck in my mind. Those big brown eyes that stared back at me. Her pale lips pressed together to hide the pain. A mass of dark brown lock whirled around her slender body. Of course, she wasn't perfect like most of us, but I couldn't shake the urge to make her mine. Yet I knew she would never be. Her wrist was cut like a cat's claw. I knew right away who did it. My sister was her mistress now. Who was I to claim the girl? The thought stung my heart. What was wrong with me?

~*~

AVERY

A bang on the wooden door of my room shook me wide awake. A man shouted from the other side as I stirred to life again.

"Get up now!" he yelled. "Get ready and go down to the dining hall. It's breakfast time."

I cleaned myself and got dressed in my maid clothing as was instructed. And we were the breakfast. The vampires would drink our blood first thing in the morning.

In turn, they feed us food.

I went downstairs and was herded to the kitchen. There were other slaves waiting there. They each had a white bandage on their wrists. A tray of wine glasses filled with fresh blood was on the marble island along with other delicacies.

"You get this to my lady." A man wiggled his finger at me. "Don't make her wait."

I collected myself before taking the tray to the dining hall. I could smell the metallic scent from the glasses, and I wanted to gag.

When I reached the hall, I waited at a white long table. Then I heard the sound of heels clicking against the floor. I dared not to raise my face to see who was coming. I sort of already knew.

From the corner of my eyes, the woman moved so gracefully, she reminded me of a stealthy panther. All her movements were consistent and elegant as she took a seat at the head of the table and crossed her long legs.

"Oh, that's my new pet," the same silky voice that had frightened me spoke. It made my body shiver. I lowered my gaze with a wince, but I could still feel her piercing stare on me.

"Come here," she said. "I need my drink."

My feet felt wobbly and my body began to tremble.

"Are you deaf?" one of the vampires hissed at me. "Serve the lady now!"

I jumped and quickly walked towards her. She wore a black knitted blazer and a white cotton blouse with an open neck. The lady of this house was this beautiful being. There was no doubt about it.

I was trying my hardest not to drop anything. My wrist was already healed. There remained only some pink scars, which were hardly visible. It was strange how a vampire bite healed so fast.

But when I put the wine glass down next to my mistress, she seized my hand. I gasped out loud.

"I forgot to mention that I need a warm fresh drink."

She gave me an amused look. Then she pulled me to her and twirled my body around. Before I knew it, I was sitting on her lap like a three-year-old. She locked me with one arm around my waist. Her free hand came up to grip my jaw, forcing me to look at her. I stared into her beautiful golden eyes. Her full breasts pressed against my upper arm. I felt my cheeks burn hot with embarrassment. The other vampires left the hall as if they already knew their cue to leave us in privacy.

"What are you doing?" I said through my locked jaw.

"Having my breakfast, why?" She said, raising an eyebrow innocently. The sound of my frantic heart must have delighted her as she kept smiling.

"Why me?" Tears welled up in my eyes.

"Are you not aware that you're far more delicious than the rest of your fellow humans?" She tossed her chin to the stirring red blood in the wine glasses.

"Fine," I hissed. "Take whatever you want."

"Good girl," she said and turned my body over so I was facing her. She leaned into my neck. I felt her other hand slither under my short skirt. Her cold fragrant breath brushed against my bare throat. Soon I felt her lips parted over my skin. My body started trembling. I squeezed eyes shut, waiting for the two tips of her sharp canine teeth. When I felt their edges, a chilling sensation went through my body.

I braced myself for the horrible pain.

But then a familiar voice broke the silence.

"Stop that, Alexandra!"

CHAPTER 5

I jolted back in surprise, but my mistress kept a firm grip on me and pulled my body closer against her. It was almost too hard for me to breathe. The more I pushed her away, the tighter her hold became. It was no use. She was a vampire. She was too strong. All I could do was fidget in her arms like a helpless prey. Once you're in the hand of a predator, you cannot escape.

Anastasia stepped towards us. Her face was so intense; it almost looked pained. I had no clue what she was thinking, but I already felt disgusted with myself.

"Morning, baby sister," Alexandra said without turning her face away from me. "You want to join the breakfast with me?" Her eyes still lingered on the area of my throat. She smoothed my hair like I was her adorable pet. My mistress was enjoying her little show she was creating with me. I looked away, biting my lips not to cry.

"Let her go, Alex," the younger woman said, sounding almost like a growl. "Aren't you ashamed of yourself trying to take advantage of a helpless human?"

"I'm not taking advantage of her," Alex said with a casual shrug. "She agreed."

Her word made my face turn red with humiliation. I did agree to let her take my blood. What else could I do as a slave?

"It didn't look like that to me," Anastasia argued.

"Tell me one good reason why I shouldn't hurt this girl, sister."

Anastasia seemed taken aback. Her golden eyes glittered in hesitation as if she was searching for the right answer. It was typical for them to do that to us, humans. We all knew that. Yet it was the first time I had heard a vampire defending me.

"This is not a slaughterhouse, sister. You can't do whatever you want with people. You have to know that this is wrong!"

My mistress burst out laughing. Then she moved me off her lap, and we both stood up. I couldn't bring myself to look at Anastasia while her sister was literally breathing down my neck. My heart pounded in my chest like a tribal drum.

"Is that all?" Alexandra said, "Then watch this."

She tilted my head to the side, and I felt a sharp pain pierced through my neck. Her fangs bit down on me like a vicious snake's. My scream echoed in the hall. I felt my blood drawn out of my veins.

"No!"

I didn't see but I heard a crashing sound and the air whizzed past my ear. Then I was released from the piercing pain. My knees buckled to the floor. The world spun around me. I could feel the warm liquid streaming down my shoulder. I pressed my hand against the wound and looked up to find Anastasia pinning her sister against the wall. Her hands clutched around Alex's throat.

"I told you to let the girl go!" she hissed in fury.

For the first time, I caught a glimpse of Anastasia's white sharp teeth snapping at her older sister. Her eyes were burning like furious flames. But Alexandra merely smirked as if the threat had no effect on her.

Then she effortlessly pried Ana's hands off.

"You like my human slave, don't you?" my mistress said, which surprised me. Anastasia just stood there blinking hard. Then she released her sister and stepped back. Her head turned to me as I was sitting on the floor with a blood-soaked shirt.

"Can't you see that, Anastasia?" Alex whispered beside her sister. "I'm telling you, her blood is richer than the god's nectar. Her scent can raise the demons in your gut all the way from hell. I can see it in your eyes. You want to feed off her just as savagely as I do. It's in our nature, sister. Why are you holding back? Go on, I promise you won't regret it."

For a moment, Anastasia's face went blank as if she was under an evil spell. Her eyes shone from bloodlust as she looked at the red oozing from my neck. But then she clenched her jaw and squeezed her eyes shut. Her fangs restricted and when she opened her eyes again, there was calmness in them.

"Just go, Avery," she said in a low voice, I almost couldn't hear it. Alex stood there with a confused frown on her face, but some sort of recognition registered in her mind.

But I didn't wait to be told twice. I picked myself up frantically then hurried out of the hall.

Chapter 6

I turned around to my sister after Avery left. Her annoying smirked made me want to slap it off her face.

"I happened to sense something strange here," Alex said with a teasing tone. "What makes you so stupid to turn down my offer? Oh wait...but I already know—"

"Stop it!" I spat. "It's none of your business."

"It's not?" she said. "Well, then make sure it remains as such with mine as well."

She looked at me like I was still a pathetic little child. I knew Alexandra wasn't someone you wanted to cross. She was stronger and faster than me. It was because she would never think twice about killing people for blood. I loathed her appetite. I loathed it as much as I loathed mine.

"A person is not a doll you can pass around as you please," I said through my clenched teeth.

"If you don't like that, fine, then no one can touch my doll," Alex said with a satisfied grin. "She's mine and mine alone. I'll torture her and I'll feed off her— and if I'm bored enough, I might turn her."

"Don't you dare, Alexandra!" I snarled, stepping up to her again. "She's suffered enough without her family. Can't you stop inflicting pain on someone weaker than you?"

"Because that's who we are, Anastasia," Alex said. "We're the superior ones. Not those filthy humans anymore! We're meant to rule over them now. Stop wasting your time protecting those people. Have you forgotten what they did to our family?"

Her words brought a cold chill to my bones. My thoughts froze as if someone had pushed the shut button. We hadn't talked about it for a long time. The images of our family— locked up in a small cramped room and humiliated by revolutionary soldiers. The day we were escorted to the field and shot dead in cold blood. It all rushed back into my mind like a fresh current of a raging river. I turned my face away with a flinch.

"It's in the past now," I said at last.

"Yes, the past that still can come alive in my mind," Alexandra said, tapping her temple. "I will make them pay with their blood. Just mark my word."

"Sister..."

But Alexandra already walked away.

~*~

AVERY

I had a nightmare for the first time since I had been here. I kept seeing my father and mother being tossed around in our hiding place. They begged for mercy, but none of those black-coated vampires had ears to listen. I was screaming, but it was like my voice got lost in the wind. I felt as if I was trapped inside a glass box, leaving the horrible scenes undisturbed.

Then I felt someone's hands pulled me into a warm cuddle. My nightmare began to fade. I gripped on to that person, believing it was my mother. I heard her whispering soothingly in my ear. I thought my nightmare had ended. And that I was actually in our hiding place, and all those vampires were nothing but my own imagination.

I opened my heavy eyelids and found two bright golden eyes looking down at me. It took a few seconds until I figured out that my reality was an actual nightmare. It wasn't a dream. The realization shocked me and saddened at the same time. But the sight of the blonde girl distracted me.

"Anastasia!" I said in a croaky voice and sat up. The blonde vampire did the same.

"You were having a nightmare, and I just..." she said but then trailed off.

"Why are you in my room?" I asked, staring at her in confusion.

"I just wanted to see if you're alright," she said. "I'm sorry about what happened with my sister this morning."

Her bright eyes stared at the cut on my neck. There were two raw spots and red bruise that would be healed the next day. It was how vampire bites were. Their saliva contained special chemicals that could heal the wound, leaving no evidence on the victim.

"You don't have to," I said. "It doesn't matter."

"But it does to me," Ana said, looking seriously stressed. She pinched the bridge of her nose and turned back to me again. "Look, Avery, I have to warn you something about Alexandra. She is as cruel as she is beautiful. Whatever she does to you, don't let it control your heart."

"Like that would make any difference," I said. "I'm a slave, remember?"

"No, Avery," she said with a shake of her head. "Don't let that change you. You're not an object."

"That is funny coming out from a vampire like you," I said. "Why are you trying to help me? Don't you want my blood, too?"

Anastasia dropped her gaze and then she stood up. Her blonde hair looked pale gold against the moonlight that peered through my window. She turned back to me again with a saddened face.

"I don't know, Avery. For the first time in my life, you're the only person I want to drink from," she said truthfully. "But that's not why I help you. There's something more—something about you…"

But she didn't finish her sentence. Anastasia then crept onto my bed. I recoiled instinctively, but she raised her hand to soothe me. Then she leaned forward until our faces were almost touching. I could smell her delicious breath in my nostrils. Her golden irises were too deep as if she had seen too much in her life. I stared back into those mesmerizing eyes. They were framed with long thick lashes that curved upward like the tail of a peacock.

"Be still," she whispered. "I need to know something."

And just like that, Ana pressed her soft lips against mine. A burst of shock ran through my whole being like electricity. I went numb from the head down. Her lips were so tender and so smooth. I had to fight the urge to move over them, part those full lips and slip my tongue inside. In fact, I would have done so if I hadn't heard a low hiss coming from her chest. Then her kiss left me.

I felt light-headed and confused.

"I'm sorry," Anastasia said with a wild expression. She turned her face away as if to hide something, but I already knew what it was. Her sharp fangs had already extracted just slightly past her red lips. I realized she was making a great effort even to kiss me.

"Ana..?"

"I must go," she said and then left the room in one big blur.

I sat on my bed blinking to myself. Some part of me tried to take in what had just happened between us, but the rest of me still couldn't function yet.

CHAPTER 7

Many days passed in a seemingly peaceful succession. I had gotten to know some other slaves in the mansion. One of them told me about how she was separated from her brother, who was put into the human farm. I wondered what was like living in the factory, but then again I didn't want to find out. This morning things were quite the same. We got our wrists cut as usual, except me. Then the vampire, who we first met, came up to me in the kitchen. He dressed in his elegant clothes as I had remembered.

For a moment, his violet eyes seemed to linger on my face longer than necessary.

"You," he said. His pale stony face held high. "From now on, you're assigned to serve whenever my mistress sends for you."

My heart sank further than it usually did. What could I say about that? Nothing. I had no choice but to nod in acceptance. Obviously, this piece of information depressed me even more.

"Now hurry up, take the blood with you," he said, beckoning to me. I picked up my tray and followed him.

At the dining hall, I saw my mistress and Anastasia were already there. They sat at the same table but far away from each other as if they couldn't bear to breathe the same air. I walked slowly towards them. The one, who bit me, didn't look at me, and neither the one who kissed me. I tried to imitate a robot, pushing all emotions out of my mind.

Emotions are bad when you are a slave. They don't help you anything but make you more miserable.

I put the wine glasses down in the middle of the table. But I had a dilemma of who I should serve first. Then I stole a glance at the quiet Ana. She was having a piece of toast and jam. I had to look again to see if it was actual jam, the kind humans would eat.

Can vampires eat human food, too? I thought. I had only heard about their blood lust and savagery. This small innocent part of their existence confused me.

"Sit down," A familiar voice said, but I didn't know whom it came from at first. Then I realized Alexandra was looking at me. A flicker of mischief gleamed from her golden eyes.

"Y-yes?" I gulped.

"I said sit down." She gestured to the chair next to her.

Even Ana looked up from her plate to us. Her porcelain skin seemed to flush a little under the tension. I gingerly took a seat as instructed. My mistress turned her face to me and smiled kindly.

"Have you heard about your new position from Victor?" she asked. I didn't know who Victor was, but I assumed he must be the wax-looking vampire who came to me last morning, so I nodded back.

"Good, now you will have to stay near me," she said. "And even eat with me."

I looked up with questions orbited around my head, but I couldn't tell if Alex was joking. Then she got up and walked towards me. Anastasia looked on from where she was with uneasy eyes. Her hand clutched the spoon, and I saw it starting to bend out of shape. Alex took another seat near my chair and pushed a glass of blood towards me. I stared at the wine glass with red liquid stirring inside and then looked back at Alex.

"I want you to drink this," she said. My eyes went wide with shock.

"Sister," Ana said with a heavy tone.

"Relax, I'm just teaching her something," my mistress said then she turned to me again. "Drink it."

"What?" I found my voice again.

"You heard me."

"No, I won't."

Suddenly, her hand grabbed the back of my neck. Her cold fingers entangled my hair as she pulled my head slightly backward. Ana rose up from her seat.

"Stay out of it!" My mistress yelled and pointed a finger at her sister. "Or I will make it worse."

Anastasia gritted her teeth, but she didn't dare to move. Somehow I felt it had something to do with my safety than her sister's threat. Alexandra turned to me again.

"You want to drink the blood from this glass, or you want me to drink the blood from you?" Alex hissed at my ear. Her nose traced over my hot cheek. Tears ran down my face as I shut my eyes and reached out to take the wine glass. My hand shook so bad, I almost dropped it.

Alex released me and smiled in encouragement.

I brought the glass lip to mine. The smell was almost unbearable, it sickened me. I tried to hold my breath and took a plunge. The red blood flowed into my mouth like poison. The coppery taste quickly enveloped my tongue and traveled down my throat. I heaved nauseously in the process, but Alexandra caught my hand and forced me to keep drinking until the glass was empty.

I dropped the glass down on the table and clutched my throat in disgust.

"Good girl." Alex beamed brightly.

"Why are you doing this to me?" I asked between sobs.

"I want you to remember this taste," she said and smiled, "because someday you will change your mind about it."

"Enough of that!" cried Anastasia from across the table. "If you want to punish her, you already have. Just leave her alone!"

She was breathing hard. I could see the pulse on her neck beating. Alex stood up and placed her hands on my shoulders. She kissed the top of my head before I could flinch away.

"You're jealous?" Alex said with a mockery leer. "Well, you should be. I've found a rare gem here. And I'll polish her up. She won't be rough like this for long."

My mistress tracked her cold fingertips down my cheek. The hair on my arms stood on ends.

"Please, Alexandra," Ana turned into a pleading tone, "I beg you. She's just a child."

"Innocent and pure," My mistress agreed. "Just the way I like it."

Anastasia rushed forward in a flash, but my mistress grabbed me by the hand and pulled me to her. She was already behind my back when Ana reached us.

"Oh, I wouldn't do that if I were you," My mistress said as her hand wrapped around my neck. "Step back or I'll snap her pretty little neck."

Ana bared her white teeth and hissed like a wildcat. The way her eyes stared at her sister would have sent any human running. But as she looked at me, being helpless in Alexandra's hand she turned away, defeated. My mistress leaned over my shoulder and whispered into my ear.

"See? No one can touch you, my little doll," she said. "I still have another game for us, but instead of playing dress up, let's play undress."

Upon hearing that, Anastasia's face snapped back at us. Her face was filled with shock. She wanted to do something, but she knew she couldn't. Her eyes looked at me as if it was going to be the last time.

"Come on, sweet girl," My mistress said to me. "We're not going to do it in this room. Someone is having trouble controlling her jealousy."

Not until then that the terror began to seep into my consciousness. A panic coursed up from the pit of my stomach. Alexandra dragged me by my elbow. I turned to Anastasia for help, but she looked like she was lost on another planet. She just stood there like one of those a marble statue, looking dazed.

As we were leaving that room, I felt like I was being sucked into a black hole and could never come back.

CHAPTER 8

I was in my mistress's room again. It was colder than I had remembered, or it could be just my own instinctive fear that made me shiver all over. Alexandra pulled me inside after she locked the huge heavy door.

I glanced around in panic, but as usual, all the windows were tightly shut. No escape route anywhere. I felt like a trapped rat waiting for the cat to gut me alive. Alexandra turned her perfect figure to look at me again. She smiled with a glint of wickedness in her eyes.

"Don't even think about —"

I ran to the small library as fast as my feet could take me then slammed the door shut and locked it.

"Wow, you must have been a marathon runner," Alexandra mocked from the other side of the room. I saw her slender figure through the stained glass of the door. I waited with a pounding heart. Then her hand burst right through the glass like it was made of paper. Shards of crystals flew all over the floor. I stepped back with a scream. My mistress turned the doorknob and opened it.

Her tall figure walked in like a graceful leopard. I tried to gulp down the lump in my throat and turned to run again, but Alex was already in my face as fast as the wind. Her strong hands grabbed me by my shoulders and shoved me against the bookshelf so hard; I saw black stars dancing in my vision. My hands gripped onto the shelf so that I wouldn't fall.

"Run all you want, but you can't hide from me," she said. "Geez, how I enjoy the game of hide-and-seek with you, Avery."

"Kill me!" I hissed. "I can't stand this anymore. Just get it over with!"

"It's not that easy, my lovely doll," Alex said, stepping closer until her body pressed against mine. She leaned her face towards mine. Her breath brushed faintly against my flushed cheeks.

"Why me?" I whispered in despair.

"Why you? I don't know." Alex raised her hand to brush a strand of hair from my face. "Besides, I like to see the effect you have over my little sister. She seems so smitten by your human charms, doesn't she?"

"At least, she's not horrible and cold-hearted like you!"

Once the words flew out of my mouth, I realized I had hit her nerves. My mistress's glowing eyes flared up like molten gold. I had to flinch away from their intensity.

"Indeed, I am far more evil and violent," she snapped in my face, "and like it or not, you're going to receive all of it!"

I thought she was about to bite me again, but then she crashed her perfect crimson lips to mine. And less than a heartbeat, her tongue was inside my mouth, slithering around like a sleek serpent.

My eyes went wide in confusion. Her hands started feeling all over my trembling body. My breath turned into whimpers. I tried to push her away, but she was too strong. My mistress slid her hand down and forcefully lifted my thigh up to her waist. Her other hand tore open the collar of my shirt, baring my shoulder and neck. The shredding sound of fine linen snapped me out of my fear.

I just can't let her do that to me.

With all my human strength, I shoved her hard enough to slip myself out of her hands and ran out of the library.

I ran past the black piano by the balcony. Before I could go any farther, I felt two strong arms wrapped around my waist and lifted me off the carpeted floor. I kicked and thrust around only to find myself landed on the grand bed. My head twirled from the impact.

"So you want to play it rough, huh?" Alex said. "Fine! I can do that."

She got on top of me, pinning my hands to my sides.

"Remember when I asked you if you liked my bed?"

"I hate your bed!"

Alexandra let out a thrilling laugh. "With the pleasure I'm about to give you, you will wish to sleep on it every night."

Then her lips and frenzy tongue found their ways into my mouth again. I struggled but then began to feel helpless. It didn't matter how hard I fought, she would always get what she wanted. Tears streamed down the corner of my eyes as my body started to go limp with exhaustion. Alex released my lips and proceeded to nuzzle my throat and went down to my breasts. I lay panting while her hands slithered over my legs and slipped inside my skirt. I could feel her razor-edged teeth brushed lightly over my skin. Then I heard myself sobbing louder.

"Shhh!" Alex hushed. She turned my face to hers and looked into my eyes. "Don't cry. It's going to be fine. It will be the most wonderful thing you've ever experienced, I promise."

With her golden eyes bore deeply into mine, I felt my heartbeat slow down. Her cold musky breath calmed my raging nerves for some reasons. It seemed like something about her soothing tone had softened me. My mistress smiled a dazzling smile as she noticed my body's reaction. She kissed my forehead, my lips, and trailing to my throat. She lingered there. I knew deep in my heart that she would feed on me again. Her canines slide out longer and sharper like the claws of a cat. They traced over my neck for the right vein.

A shiver shot through my spine. Then there was a sting like the jab of two needles. But the pain was over quickly and replaced by indescribable bliss. The vampire's venom could heighten a victim if chose to. And I felt a strange sensual feeling rushed into my system. My back arched with an unidentified pleasure.

I felt a hot stirring between my legs. My body began to melt like lava as she started grinding herself against me. A moan issued from my trembling lips. I felt confused and embarrassed to like the sensation. I wished I could have let myself go and given in to this newfound lust. I wished I could have forgotten everything, yet a soft gentle voice in the back of my head broke out like a burst of bubbles, *'Don't let her control you.'*

Then I remembered Ana's caring face. Her soft moistened lips and deep sad eyes. The thought of her brought me a new surge of strength. My drowsy eyelids flew open again, and I pushed Alex's heavy form off of me. With a quick glance, I could see her face marred with a surprise. I desperately rolled myself out of bed and dropped to the floor.

"Avery!" my mistress cried.

My mind was still heavily intoxicated, but I forced my body to move.

Staggering to my feet again, I stumbled and rushed towards the door. The chance of me escaping from her was as slim as the chance to stay alive in a world full of new bloodthirsty species, but I didn't care anymore.

My legs dragged me as far as the main room until I felt a hand pulled me back by the hair. Another hand gripped me by my jaw hard.

"What is wrong with you?!" Alexandra hissed furiously. "Nobody has ever rejected me!"

"Because I'm a human!" I spat back. "And I hate everything about you!"

With a surge of anger, I grabbed her hand that held my face and bit into it as hard as I could. My mistress cried out in pain. She drew her hand back and then slapped me across the face.

I fell on the floor and tasted blood in my mouth.

Suddenly, I heard a loud bang on the door, making the hinges rattled by the force. Another bang and the door flung open. Anastasia marched into the room.

One glance at me on the floor with blood dripping from the corner of my mouth, she darted out like a lightning towards her sister. They both rammed into each other and flew across the room, smashing into the walls and glass windows.

Alexandra pushed back and they went deadlock, hurling themselves onto the piano. There were chaotic noises echoed up the ceiling. But it seemed my mistress was a lot stronger than her sister.

After a few minutes of struggling, she managed to throw Anastasia through the air. Her sister's back smashed into the far wall, and she collapsed onto the floor again. White plasters fell like snowflakes all around her lying form.

"Anastasia!" I cried and staggered back to my feet.

"You're not the golden child in the family anymore, Anastasia," Alex said. She raised her hand, her fingernails flashed into claws, aiming at her sister. "I'll teach you a few lessons about respect."

I reached Anastasia at the same time Alex did.

Before she could lash out at her sister, I threw myself and shielded her body from the deadly hand. Alex's nails slashed through the thin layer of my cotton shirt like a lioness's. They sliced the skin on my back open like knives.

I let out a painful cry.

"No! Avery, oh no, no!" I heard Ana's voice scream. She crawled to my side as I fell to the floor. Alex's eyes widened as if she couldn't comprehend what she just did. My mistress stood staring at us with my blood dripping from her fingers.

Ana lifted my limp body off the floor and rested my head on her chest.

"Alex, how could you do this? You're a monster!" she yelled. For a moment, I saw my mistress flinched. I couldn't speak due to the pain and shock. Then as if it was natural, Anastasia bit her own wrist and brought it to my lips.

"Please, please, drink it, Avery, it'll help you," she insisted when I turned my head away with a wince. "I'm so sorry."

She pressed the bleeding gash to my mouth. I expected to taste the metallic taste again, but her vampire blood was rich and different from the human blood. Its distinct taste was unbelievably addictive.

I drank and drank until my vision went black.

Chapter 9

That's funny.

Why do I even bother to think about it? It's not like I have never killed before. Avery Pierce is just an inferior and stubborn human girl. She deserved to be punished. I don't see why I shouldn't torture her. The sound of her screams delights me. Her blood whispers to me. But then there is something I couldn't wrap my mind around. Why did I feel like there were insects crawling inside my stomach when I saw her and my sister together? And why of all the whys, why do I want to have Avery more than anything now?

~*~

AVERY

I woke up to the bright sunlight shining through an open window. Silk curtains flickered in the morning breeze. There was a breathtaking view of the mountain outside. This wasn't my little room in the mansion. The walls were wooden and polished smooth. There were paintings hanging around the place. I could see flowers blossoming in tiny buckets on every sill of the windows.

"Oh, you're awake," a familiar voice said. I turned around to see Anastasia smiling at me. She was holding a plate of sandwich and a glass of milk.

"What is this place?" I sat up and looked around myself.

"My house."

"Your house?"

"It's my vacation house actually," she said. "I like to come here whenever I want to be alone."

"It's so beautiful," I said. My eyes wandered out the window. A pristine lake with green forest stretched far into the distance.

"I'm glad you like it here," Ana said and put the food down on a small wooden table next to my bed.

"What happened? Why did you bring me here?"

"Now you eat first, questions later," she just said. "You're still recovering."

My back felt fine. I turned my head over my shoulder, trying to see my injury and feel it with my hands, but the wound was gone. I didn't know how I could heal so fast, but then I remembered when Ana let me drink her blood.

"Your blood cured me?" I said.

She nodded.

I had heard about it in legend, but I never thought it was true. With a sigh, I reached out for the glass of fresh milk and took a sip. I realized how hungry I was until then. Ana watched me with steady eyes. For a moment, I started to worry about how I looked. Ana, as usual, was immaculate without an effort. Her silky blonde hair almost looked like strands of woven gold. It framed her perfect angular face and cascaded down her lithe form. Anastasia was undoubtedly more beautiful than any other vampires I'd met— aside from her cruel sister, of course.

"You're very brave, Avary," she said. "I've never seen anyone who stood against my sister like that."

"No wonder why I was rewarded with her claws," I said, glancing over to my back again. Anastasia let out a melodious laugh. I had to stop chewing on my sandwich just to listen to it. Her face became serious again.

"I'm sorry, Avery," she said. "It was my fault. I shouldn't have let you go with her."

"So why did you come back for me then?" I said, trying not to be upset with her.

"I just couldn't stop thinking about you," she said. "It's killing me."

"It's killing me too, literally," I found myself speaking louder than I had meant to.

"I know." Ana looked down. "I am so sorry for all of that happened."

"No, please, it's not your fault. Anyway, how come you brought me here?" I asked to change the subject. "How about your sister?"

"Don't worry, Alex doesn't know this place," she said. "You're safe with me."

"Really?"

She nodded.

Then a thought popped into my mind. "Ana, I mean...Anastasia..."

"Call me Ana," she said. "I like the way you call me that."

"Oh alright, I was meaning to ask you, when you saved me from Alex didn't it bother you when I was bleeding in your hands?"

"Well," she breathed and stood up. "I don't know how it could be possible, but the moment I saw you on the floor bleeding, my heart just stopped. All I could think of was you. Not the bloodlust, not the hunger. Just you."

I looked up at her and then we held each other's gaze. We broke our eye contact off after a while.

"I think I better get changed," I said. But Ana muffled a laugh. I frowned at her

"What?"

"Sorry," she said. "But I already changed your clothes."

"You what?" I cried then looked down at myself. I was wearing a white cotton shirt two sizes bigger than me and a pair of black panties, which was mine. But I resisted the urge to look if I wore any bra. I already knew I didn't.

"I know the shirt is a bit too big. It's my painting shirt," Ana said, reading my face. "I wear it for comfort."

"Oh, it's not...that," I said. "Wait, you paint?"

"Yes, a little bit," she said with a shrug. Then I looked around the room again. Every wall hung beautiful art pieces that looked like they were fresh from the national museum or some art gallery.

"Oh my," I said. "You're an artist."

I got out of bed and took a private tour around the place, devouring each work with my eyes. The whole time, Anastasia watched me in silence.

"This is brilliant!" I gasped.

"You like art, too?" Ana came to stand beside me.

"I don't understand much about art, but I love it anyway," I said, "Before the war started, my father used to take me and my brother to art exhibitions. My mother liked music more, though."

"Oh, music," Ana echoed my word, but I heard a strange tone in it as if she was thinking of something or someone. Then I realized without her telling me.

"Your sister likes music, right?" I asked. "I saw her piano."

"She's a genius," Ana said in a matter of fact way. "Whenever the palace held a celebration, she would play to entertain the guests. But she's never played it again ever since we—"

She didn't finish her sentence. And I didn't ask.

Ana turned and smiled at me sadly. I didn't know what to say to that, so I kept moving on. Then I almost bumped into a wooden easel by the window. A white cloth covered the piece.

"What is this one?" I said, reaching for the cover and opened it.

"Oh, it's nothing," Ana tried to say, but I already uncovered it. Behind the white cloth was a picture of me sleeping on the bed.

I recognized myself immediately since the drawing was breathtakingly perfect and realistic. It was like staring at a black and white photograph. Except the girl in the picture looked so peaceful and innocent as if nothing horrible had happened in her life.

"Why did you draw me?" I said, staring at the picture in admiration. I traced my fingers along the fine gray lines of the pencil.

"You just turned beautiful when you were asleep," she said with a smile. "Like the angel I'd always wished to draw."

My face reddened. I bit my lips from smiling.

"I didn't know you're a poet, too," I mocked her. She laughed again and it was a joyful tone that I laughed along.

Then we stopped and looked at each other. Anastasia came forward and smoothed my dark brown lock gently. Her golden eyes sparkled with hidden feelings.

She slipped her hands around my waist and cautiously pulled my body closer. My heart pounded, my breath shortened, but it wasn't from fear, it was out of anticipation and pure bliss. I had never felt like this with anyone.

I longed for those perfect scented lips to touch mine again. And when she leaned her face slowly, I couldn't wait and went out to meet her half way. There our lips touched and merged with tenderness. A second later, our tongues wrestled in and out hungrily. The kiss was passionate and pure, and I felt so loved.

As our bodies seemed to crave one another, writhing rhythmically like two entwined serpents, I slipped my hands under her silk blouse, feeling the soft cold body. She moved down to kiss my neck. Her tongue licked the skin above my breasts.

But then she pulled herself away from me and turned her face to the window.

"Ana, what's wrong?" I asked with a frown.

"I'm sorry, Avery," she said. "I can't do this."

"Why not?" I said, deeply upset and hurt. "If you don't want me, why did you make me feel this way about you?"

"Avery, can't you see me what I am?" Ana turned her face back, her canine teeth flashing white and sharp. "I'm a monster! That's what I am!"

I didn't recoil like I used to. She wanted to scare me away, but I did not care.

"No, you're wrong. You're not like your sister. You're my guardian angel, Anastasia," I said and walked over to her. I turned her body around to face me. Her canines were long and sharp, yet strangely beautiful. They seemed to fit her angelic face naturally.

"I know it's much too soon, but I don't know how much time I have left in this cruel world. I need to ask you before it's too late. It's my last wish. Will you fulfill it?" I whispered.

"Avery, I would do anything for you," she said.

"Then I want you to take me, Anastasia. I want you to take me all the way."

She looked at me for a long time. Then I grabbed her face and kissed her hard on the lips. She pried me off, but I held onto her tightly, pulling her to my desperate embrace. A moment later, I felt her tensed body began to loosen up. The sharp edges of her teeth disappeared. Then we kissed slowly this time.

When we parted again, she looked at me with soft golden eyes.

"You have no idea how much I crave you, Avery," she said.

"Take me," I whispered.

Anastasia bit her bottom lip, but I could feel her burning desire coursing within her, melting her resolve.

Then ever so slowly, she nodded.

CHAPTER 10

ANASTASIA

Avery's big brown eyes shone with a deep longing that I couldn't refuse it. We walked hand in hand back to the bed and sat there facing each other. I kept staring at her doll-like face, so innocent and so adorable. My gaze made her blush bright red.

She looked down, hiding her eyes under those long black lashes. The wind blew through the windows. Silk curtains flicked gently, making the only sound in the room.

Then Avery looked up again and moved closer until our knees touched. She swallowed hard before reaching her hands over to unbutton my shirt, but I knew she was nervous. Her hands were shaking so much; I had to grab them in mine.

"It's alright," I reassured her. "I won't hurt you."

"I know. It's just that…" she said, looking back at me with that beautiful face. "I just want to do it right. I want it to be perfect."

"Avery, I can make you happy."

"I know," She said. Then she came onto my lap, straddling me. Our faces were only inches away. Her flat stomach faintly brushed against my chest. My arms wrapped around her dainty waist. I stroked her small back underneath the oversized shirt. Her body was so warm and soft. I couldn't ignore the appetizing smell of her skin, it was so overwhelming. Without realizing myself, I inhaled her sweet delicious scent. Avery was still looking at me, and for a moment, she seemed to understand. It was still hard to control my thirst, my everlasting thirst for her fresh youthful blood.

"I'm sorry," I said, looking away in shame.

"You can drink from me, Ana, I don't mind," she said, snapping me out of my bloodlust.

"What are you talking about, Avery? I won't feed on you just like that!" I said. Avery stroked my hair. Her arms wound around my shoulders as she leaned to whisper in my ear.

"It's not called feeding if I let you. We're just creating a bond together," she said and planted butterfly kisses on my cheek and neck. "I want to give you everything, my blood, my virginity and—my heart."

A veil of happiness enveloped me. Her touch was electrifying. My skin tingled with her welcoming warmth. How could that be possible? For so many decades, I had never felt so powerless. This girl invaded my mind. She slipped into my every thought and filled up my soul with too many emotions. My heart felt like it might burst from the joy she'd given me. She brought life to my empty existence.

Yet, the flow of her blood was like a siren's call to me. It had always been inviting me from the first day I met her. I looked up at her again. Avery gave a sweet innocent smile.

"Please, don't push it, Avery, I—" I said but she brought her soft lips to mine, cutting me off.

The tenderness of her mouth set my thoughts astray. My mind whirled at the touch of her delicious taste.

I found myself kissing her back, slowly but passionately. Her hands ran through my hair, her hips began to move instinctively over me, arousing me.

Her tongue gave a slight silky brush over my upper teeth. I opened my mouth for her. A familiar sensation made my jaw throb. Then she broke off and moved down to nuzzle my neck.

"Bite me, Anastasia," Avery whispered between kisses. Her head tilted for me.

"Avery..." I tried to speak, but I was short of breath myself. My heart, which was frozen cold for so long started to pound wildly again.

"Please," she said again and unbuttoned her shirt one by one, peeling off the silk layer, revealing her glowing skin. The sight of her bared shoulders and her healthy form only made my thirst grow stronger. She hugged me tight, urging me on. I couldn't stand it anymore. My lips pulled over my teeth. Instantly, the muscle around my jaw squeezed the sharp white canines out of my gum, and I let them sink into Avery.

She winced a little. Then her body relaxed, drowning in with a rush of endorphin-like venom I was giving her. Her sweet blood burst into my mouth, flowing down my throat. It was so warm and so delicious. A thousand words couldn't describe the taste of it. I almost forgot myself. But it wasn't long before I forced myself to pull away. I stared at Avery's face. She got those dreamy eyes as we looked at each other. I gave her a dazed smile and claimed her lips again with my blood stained mouth. I could tell Avery was high from my bite. I was high from bloodlust myself. The sexual craving also grew more intense between us.

And I figured it was the time that we should do something about it.

I swiftly turned us over and lay Avery down onto the bed. She giggled with a fit of excitement. I got on top of her, smiling. Avery's hands rose up and pulled me down to her. I found my face buried in her soft delicate breasts, sucking and licking them to my heart's content.

Our bodies moved in rhythm against one another. I slipped my hand under her black panties. She gasped as my fingers reached her sensitivity, teasing her innocence with my most gentle touch. I continued sucking her nipples as my other hand squeezed and fondled Avery earnestly.

She moaned softly in her throat. I kissed her neck where I had just bitten. Goosebumps rose all over her skin. I felt her entrance get hotter and slicker. It gave me joy. I couldn't wait to explore her world. Moving down slowly, I took off her panties, taking my time. Avery bit her lips as she looked on. When her delicate body was completely naked, I stopped to admire the breathtaking view. She was indeed beautiful. It made my stomach growl with hunger, but a different kind of hunger.

I decided to get down and work the magic. I kissed her inner thigh then moved over slowly to where the wonder was about to happen.

I opened my mouth and started my first lap.

Oh god, she's so delicious.

Avery jerked from sensitivity. Her moans were heard in the quiet room. I began licking, slowly and tenderly, turning her breath into ceaseless whimpers. Her scent even got stronger as my tongue traced over her femininity. With a quick glance, I saw Avery's eyes fluttering with pleasures. Her hand gripped the pillow by her side, her other hand held onto the bed sheet. She must have sensed that she was getting close.

My hands snaked around from her thighs to hold her hips, keeping her writhing body still. Then after a few minutes of warming up, I slipped my tongue inside her. Avery gasped. Her toes curled. Her eyes flared open from a shocking ecstasy.

Her back arched as my tongue wagged all over, feeling its way around her warm slippery walls. Avery moaned loudly, gripping the bed sheet harder. I could sense a strong sensation building up. Her body blushed and began to tremble out of control. I could hear her heart beating furiously. Blood rushed backward. The warm walls were getting hotter against my mouth. The tip of my tongue rubbed every pleasurable place of her sweet flower until she was screaming.

Avery's body twisted with overwhelming sensation, ready to reach her climax. My tongue became more violent. Then she could take it no more and let out a loud cry. I felt her warm walls contracted as she came.

A cry of her orgasm satisfied me. Her stomach heaved for a full minute from her first intense release. I kissed her thighs before pulling way.

My mouth and chin were smeared with her love juices.

I licked my lips. She blushed when she saw that, but I grinned at her.

Avery motioned for me to come into her arms. We cuddled each other and stayed contented like that for the longest time.

CHAPTER 11

AVERY

The bed was empty when I woke up. An immediate anxiety washed over me as I was alone and scared.

"Anastasia!" I called out, but there was no answer. I threw off the cover and sprinted out of the bed. "Anasta..."

To my relief, she appeared into the room. But she wore nothing but a white towel wrapped around her glowing body. Her blonde hair was wet. The water droplets on skin made her glow. I froze as she came to me quickly. Her face looked concerned.

"I'm right here, Avery. Are you not well?" She brought her hands to my cheeks. I couldn't breathe, not with her in a towel was this close to me. I found myself staring at her chest. Anastasia looked down at herself and huffed.

"Oh geez, sorry, that is inappropriate. I was taking a quick bath..."

"Ana...please don't leave me like that again," I said. "I'm lost without you."

"I won't leave you, Avery, I promise," she said, stroking my cheeks with adoration.

I felt my body turn hot as if I was coming down with a fever. She was naked underneath that towel. I hadn't seen all of her yet, but the thought of having her bare and exposed did make my inside tingle with new needs.

How the hell do I want her again already?

"I think I'm in constant need of you, Anastasia," I admitted.

She looked at me. Then she smiled.

"Maybe we should kiss a little?" Ana said. I smiled back and wrapped my arms around her waist. She tucked my hair behind my ears. Her slightly damped skin smelled like fresh cut roses. Then we kissed. Her touch electrified my skin. I traced the outline of her lips with mine. Her impossibly long eyelashes fluttered. I couldn't help moaning into our kiss.

She had me.

I was totally and completely in love with her.

I pushed Anastasia to the bed and tried to remove her towel, but she kept holding onto it. We both giggled.

"Let go!" I said.

"You're an animal!" Ana laughed. I made a growling sound, which made her laugh even more. Then I got on top of her and kissed her perfect lips.

Anastasia moved her thighs between mine as I started grinding in a sensual rhythm against her private part. The motion made her face turn almost rosy red.

She finally let go of her towel. I tossed it aside, revealing her flawless body. I just couldn't believe I got to make love with this goddess. The whole thing made me tremble. The wetness between our legs became more luscious.

A strong sensual pleasure was taking shape as our bodies moved with passion. It was like all that exist was us. Ana closed her eyes when my lips and tongue found hers. Then I sat upright. Ana's hands went to my breasts and roamed over my churning body. Her brows knitted together as I pressed harder and faster. We were slippery and hot and very close. My gasps mixed with occasional moans.

Then electric sparks burst between our legs, seizing our muscles with gripping joy. All actions halted due to the blissful effect. I let out a long moan while my body convulsed. A moment later, I dropped myself over Ana again, panting as hard as she did.

"Oh geez," Ana gasped, eyes widened as she looked down. "I never thought you were that good."

"Neither did I," I smiled sheepishly and rolled off of her.

"I think I need a shower again," Ana said, "Look, I got all slippery."

"How about I join you?" I raised an eyebrow at her.

"Thought you would never ask." She smiled back.

And the shower provided us just as much pleasure.

CHAPTER 12

I wish things would stay the same forever when I was with Anastasia. We could live in our little house and be contented. There was only one problem. I had never seen her drinking human blood like Alex, but that doesn't mean she could go days without it.

I had offered her my blood, but she refused and went on a quick hunt near the mountain slope. I didn't want her to leave me alone, but I also didn't want to make it hard on her either

After Anastasia left, I stayed inside doing some mundane things around the house while I waited. Suddenly, I heard a knock on the door. My heart almost leaped out of my chest.

But excitement got the best of me. I rushed to the door and opened it.

"Ana, you came back quite early today," I said.

But standing in front of me was a strange woman. Her elegant posture erected tall and proud. She had flowing long hair as brown as mine, but her eyes were pools of vivid violet, piercing into mine.

"Who are you?" She asked me. I was still stunned by her sudden presence. Her skin was slightly paler than me and her perfect lips were as red as blood. I got the answer right away that she wasn't any fellow human.

She stared at me from head to toes. I took a few steps back. Now I was in danger of an unknown vampire. I wished Anastasia would be here soon. The woman smiled, but it wasn't a friendly smile. I yanked the door shut, but her hand that looked too delicate to be any stronger than mine pushed it aside. The door swung with a crashing sound and she stepped gracefully into the house.

"What...what do you want?" I gasped. "Who are you?"

"I was invited here...once," she said. "You haven't answered my question yet."

The woman stood in the hallway now with her arms crossed. She looked around herself as if in nostalgia. Then her head crooked to the side as she turned back to look at me. I swallowed hard before glancing at the clock. Ana told me she would be back before sunset. The sun had just dipped behind the mountain. I didn't know how long was this going to take for her to come back.

But now, I was scared.

My instinct told me to run. And run I did. Without saying a word, I turned around and started to sprint. But the vampire rushed over to me so fast, I didn't see her until she was in front of me. Her hands pushed my body against the wall of the hallway. Her cold body pressed against my back. Her hand was around my throat from behind.

"Tell me, who are you?!" she hissed in my ear. I could feel her white sharp teeth snapped near my face. My heart raced and my breathing hitched.

"My...my name...is...Avery," I said in a panic voice. "I'm...I'm a human slave of Alexandra."

"Then why are you here in this house?" She lifted my chin up higher, giving more access to the veins on my throat.

"Anastasia...brought me...here," I choked out the words. Then there was a long pause. After that, the vampire turned me around to face her, but she still kept a firm grip on me. Her bright violet eyes looked perplexed and angry as if she didn't like what she was thinking inside her head.

"She brought you here? Why did she bring you here?" she continued to question me, sounding like a bloodsucking maniac she was. "No one else was brought into this place but me!"

Her grip tightened around my throat with each word. I couldn't breathe. I tried to push her away. After a moment of hopeless struggle, she finally let me go.

I dropped to my knees, coughing.

The vampire was looking down at me. She had a malicious look on her face. Despite my fear, I managed to muster up the courage to ask her the only question had been burning inside me.

"And who are you?"

"I'm Nikol," she replied. "Anastasia's girlfriend."

CHAPTER 13

My jaw dropped. Anastasia's girlfriend? The thought stabbed at me like a blade. I felt something akin to a heart attack. I couldn't breathe. My stomach churned, and I felt as if I was about to throw up. I couldn't believe it. But the woman was standing right before my eyes. She was real, and she was here, now claiming back what was hers.

Why did Anastasia do that to me? Why she never told me she already has a lover? Maybe I was just another slave to her. Whatever we had was merely a sexual enjoyment. I was too easy to fall in love. I was too stupid to lose myself.

With the thoughts screaming in my head, hot tears streamed down my cheeks. I tried to swallow the pain, but it was too late to stop my heart from breaking.

Nikol kept staring at me with her cold eyes.

"Why are you crying?" She knelt down to look at my face. I recoiled back and wiped my eyes.

"Why didn't Ana tell me about you?" I asked. My voice cracked with sorrows.

"Don't answer me with a question, slave girl!" Nikol grabbed the back of my neck and pulled me back closer. Her breath was like a stream of fire on my face. I winced at the sight of her livid eyes. They were full of hatred and jealousy. I couldn't help shaking in fear.

"You're in love with my girlfriend, aren't you? That's why you're crying," Nikol said again. "But I'm telling you, Anastasia will never think of you more than just a human slave. You might taste good as I can smell your rich blood, but it is me, the only one she loves and always will. If you're smart, get the hell out of here before I rip you apart, do you hear me?"

I didn't know what to say. I couldn't find the words. There was nothing I could do but to bury the pain in my chest. How could Anastasia do this to me? I thought she had feelings for me, too. I felt like a thousand knives had slashed every part of my body. Why did it have to hurt so much? I sobbed louder.

Nikol released me and stood up.

"Now, go away," she said. "I won't say it twice."

With my heart felt like a heavy lead, I got up and gathered my old clothes before leaving through the front door, leaving the beautiful sanctuary and the memory of Anastasia loving me behind.

It was like a dream that was stuttered when you woke up.

I couldn't breathe any better outside. But I hugged my trembling body and ordered my feet to walk down the stony path. It was windy and cold as the nightfall had arrived.

I didn't know where I was heading, but I kept walking and walking as if I was in a trance. Until there was a flash of headlights burst into my retinas. I jumped and shielded my face with my hand.

Before I could react, several strong hands grabbed me by my arms and shoulders, forcing me towards a black limousine. I tried to kick and yell, but it was to no avail.

They shoved me into the car like a trash bag. I heard the engines of several other cars started. Doors slammed shut.

I looked around as the cars started moving.

"Surprised much?" a familiar angelic voice said. I turned back and found another person sitting by the window at the other side. Her long legs crossed. Her long silky black hair looked like raven feathers inside the dark interior of the car.

"Alexandra," I breathed.

"Good that you still remember your mistress," she said, turning her face to me at last. Under the silver glow of the moonlight, Alex was as intimidating as she was stunning. My mind went blank once we held each other's gaze. I almost forgot the miserable feeling I had a moment ago when I looked at her. Her jaw clenched and unclenched as if something was stirring deep inside her. Then in a blink of an eye, I found her cold hand gripping my chin, forcing me to look into her golden eyes.

"Don't you ever think I would never find out where you are and what you did with my sister, Avery," she hissed through teeth. "I can smell the sex on your skin. You make me feel disgusted!"

"Then don't touch me!" I snapped back. Alex's face went hard like a stone. I was waiting for the slap or the bite, but it never came.

Instead, she smashed her lips into mine and moved over them forcefully and feverishly. It was an angry kiss. She kept a firm hand at the back of my neck while her other hand squeezed my breast. It hurt me almost to tears, and I could barely breathe.

I tried to push her away, but it wasn't until she broke the kiss by herself that I could be free from the torture. There was a sting on my bottom lip and a small droplet of blood oozed out.

Alex's razor-teeth had cut me. I looked back at her in shock.

"This will remind you that you still belong to me," she said.

In that a moment, I just wanted to die and forget about everything.

CHAPTER 14

ALEXANDRA

As soon as the limo stopped in front of the mansion, I grabbed Avery by the wrist and dragged her out of the car. She almost tripped on the way but I kept walking until we reached the main hall. I turned to the guards.

"Call the maids," I said. "Bring her to clean up and get her back to my room."

"No!" Avery cried in terror, struggling with my tight grip. "Please, don't do this to me."

"Shut up!" I yelled at her. "I can't stand another minute smelling the scent of my sister on you anymore. This time I won't let you get away from me again. You'll see."

Avery winced, but she had to deal with the consequence she had caused when she left me for Anastasia. Though it wasn't entirely her fault, I was still going to punish her for sleeping with my sister.

Thinking about what they did together made my jaw clench and my teeth throb. But I wanted more to rip Ana's throat out for that. Yet I would have to tolerate this for a while, for I knew what would hurt Anastasia more than anything. I would make them both suffer as much as I did.

The maids came in and took Avery away.

After tonight, things will change, I thought to myself.

I didn't know how much time had passed. I had lost count of minutes and hours for many years. The full moon rose up high in the pitch-black sky. I sat on the armchair by the window with a wine glass in my hand. The unusual glow was no longer sickening to me. Waiting was in my nature. I always waited for the prey to forget themselves and lose in my arms. But now, I couldn't wait anymore. The anticipation was stronger than I expected, and I wanted Avery now.

Then the groan of my chamber doors sounded. I smelled the fresh lustrous scent of the girl I had been waiting for. A smile plastered on my face. I could also smell her fear and unease in every breath she took. It was almost too overwhelming for my predator senses. If it wasn't for the sake of good old civilized manners, I would have bolted out and ripped her clothes off. But I promised myself to be more patient with this girl. She wasn't an ordinary prey. I would quite like to play this game a little longer.

Putting the wine glass down, I stood up and walked towards her. Avery was wearing the red Russian silk dress I got for her. She didn't know this. The maids had fixed it so perfectly over her lovely frame. For a moment, I could do nothing but admire every part of her body. She was utterly beautiful.

Avery just stared straight back at me. She didn't show any sign of terror as I had expected. But I knew she was just trying to act tough. I appreciated her human will, but I would like to change that soon.

"You're not afraid?" I asked. She looked me into my eyes. I swear I could feel a slight twinge from her piercing stare.

"Do whatever you want," she muttered back. "I don't care anymore."

"Oh, really?" I raised an eyebrow at her.

I guessed Nikol's showing up was still a shock to Avery, but I didn't expect this. I almost felt sorry for her, yet I would love to find out how Anastasia deal with this mess later. I stepped closer to Avery, our bodies almost touched. She recoiled back a little. I smiled and stroked her adorable cheek. She didn't move.

Then I slid my hand to her waist and pulled her delicate body into my arms. My nose kept inhaling the rich scent from her soft healthy skin. I couldn't get enough of it. Avery bit her lips but a small crystal tear betrayed her. She knew she couldn't get away from me anymore. I would have her and take her tonight, no doubt. My hand smoothed her hair and wiped the tear away with my thumb.

I leaned over to her ear.

"Just forget about her," I whispered. "I can give you more than she could."

Without waiting, I pulled Avery into my tight embrace. Her warm breathing quickened. I loved the way her heart pounded against her chest. It was a summoning music to my dark soul. She whimpered when I buried my face between her neck and shoulder. The minute my lips touched her delicious skin, she started to wiggle wildly in my arms again.

I lost my patience.

"Stop it, Avery!" I hissed. "I don't want to hurt you any more than you deserve, but this is what you have to pay. You're mine!"

Avery froze with wide eyes. But I didn't wait to hear her pathetic responses and just dragged her to the bedroom.

When we reached the bed, I turned to her again.

"Get on the bed," I said.

"What?" Avery's head snapped back to me.

"I said get on the bed!"

"You're a sick psychopath vampi—"

I lifted the girl off her feet and tossed her onto the puffy bed like she weighed nothing. Avery's mouth flung open in surprise. I swiftly crawled up and locked her down under me again.

"This is it, huh?" Avery spat the words in my face, "You won't be satisfied unless you see me suffer!"

"Oh since when did you become so smart?" I said and dropped myself over her. My body wedged between her legs. Avery tried to arch her back to push me, but I kept her caged under me. My movement was smooth and quick that Avery couldn't stop my advance. By then I was lying on her desirable form with our faces inches apart. Then my lips and tongue went straight to where they belong.

Avery tried to toss her head away to escape me, but I gripped her jaw back, forcing her lips to let me in. My tongue thrust down her throat furiously. I moaned into her mouth. Yet she couldn't seem to break free from my craving kiss, and ever so slowly, Avery gave in. I heard her sob in silence. There was nothing she could do, but to let me take her all the way.

Once her petite body fell limp from exhaustion, I started stroking her beautiful breasts. My hand reached down her flat belly then went farther down to the wonderful hot place between her legs.

"Please don't...please..." she begged me to stop, squirming. Of course, I continued, stroking her down there over her silk dress, enjoying the blush on her lovely cheeks. Whether she wanted it or not, her body inevitably responded to my touch.

I kissed her throat and unfastened her red gown, revealing her soft creamy breasts. Avery panted as I started caressing them, sucking the pink nipples until they went hard.

Avery gasped and soon enough, she was shaking from the sensation. Even she was trying to hold it I could still hear her muffled moans.

This little beauty could no longer resist me.

"I know you want me, too," I whispered against her skin. Avery squirmed when I licked and teethed her all over. I shredded her panties and cupped her heated part. She gasped out loud.

My fingers already slithered over her dampened flower, gently twirling the tips around her slick opening. It caused her slippery juices to accumulate there.

Avery clenched her teeth, squeezing her eyes shut from the sensual bliss. Once she was heavily soaked through and through, I slipped inside her, so suddenly and so effortlessly.

She yelped a little in shock, yet by no means of being hurt. There was also a hint of pleasure in her cry. Avery was fully aware of her sensitive passage being filled deliciously, and she gasped again.

It was undeniable that she had to surrender to me. Without knowing it herself, her hands went to wrap around my body.

I felt her nails digging into my back, and it made me smile in triumph. She was oozing with yearning. Her hips instinctively stirred before she stopped herself.

"Alex...Alex, please..." she tried to protest in a breathless voice, but I kept moving deep inside her.

"Shhh...let it be, your teenage hormones need it," I whispered a tease in her ear. "Forget everything for a moment and just feel."

Avery tried not to roll her eyes back as I did this. I had absolute control over her. It felt so good in her soft warm cocoon. She stopped protesting and simply let me do what I wanted.

The human girl was breathing harder under me.

I began to dive a little deeper, trying to reach her weakest depth. It caused her to jaw snap open with overwhelming pleasure.

"Oh my god, Alex!"

I continued kissing her neck. My other hand squeezing and folding her blushed breasts.

Avery's hands clung tightly onto me as her legs fell open for more sensual bliss. Her hips instinctively rose from the bed, allowing me to enjoy her as much as I wanted.

Avery was losing herself to lust, I could tell by the way her head tossed and tilted between gasps. My tongue licked her breasts while my other hand exploring different pleasurable spots of her sensitive nirvana .

"Will you open your legs for me a little more?" I whispered against her blushed skin, and to my wild delight, she complied.

My palm was completely soaked with her lovely juices. Her entire body glistened with sweat. Avery couldn't even stop herself from moaning now. Her jaw dropped from the building ecstasy. Then slowly, like a waking volcano, she exploded with a cry of intense release. Avery gripped me so hard; I had to stop due to the tightness between her legs. After the moment of eruption passed, she fell back limply on the bed, panting and twitching.

I carefully pulled out of her with a victorious smile on my face.

CHAPTER 15

ANASTASIA

I carried the little creature in my arms, making sure that it wouldn't get hurt or slip away. Two long white ears popped out from the sweater I had wrapped around it. I looked down on the fluffy white ball with a smile. Avery was going to like this little fella. The rabbit twitched its small pink nose and kept staring back at me with curious eyes.

"Don't worry, little man," I said. "I won't eat you."

I walked into the house and went straight to the bedroom. The light was off, leaving only a faint glow of the moon through the window. Avery must have been tired of waiting for me. I felt bad for having to leave her alone for too long.

Maybe a fluffy pet would make her forgive me.

I walked towards the bed and saw my beloved girl lying there. A smile stretched across my face as I slowly crept forward. She would be surprised to see this.

I placed the bunny on the bed next to her. The white fluffy animal started nestling around the soft blanket. But Avery still didn't turn herself around. She was probably still sulking because I took too long to come back. I smoothed her hair and shook her shoulder gently.

"Avery, sweetheart?" I whispered. "Look at what I've got for you."

She slowly turned her head, and when my eyes met hers, I almost jumped out of my skin away from her. I stared at that too familiar face with my mouth opened. I blinked hard, wondering if she was real. That face, that beautiful charming face I could never forget.

Now, she was back.

"Hello, Anastasia. Still remember me?" She sat up and smiled warmly at me.

"Nikol," I breathed.

"I miss hearing your voice saying my name," she said and leaned towards me. "And how our lips used to lock in passionate kisses."

Shock and fear paralyzed me. Just out of the blue, my living nightmare had returned. Nikol came to wrap her arms around my neck and stared at my face with those lustful violet eyes.

"Why are you here?" I said.

"I'm here to love you again, Anastasia," she replied and then quickly kissed me full on the lips. I pushed her away and stood up.

"You're not supposed to be here!" I said and then a shocking realization hit me. I turned to grip her arms, digging my nails into her flesh.

"Where is she? What did you do to her?" I hissed furiously.

"Who?"

"You know who I'm talking about!" I yelled louder.

"Oh, you mean that pathetic-looking human girl? Well, I guess she's gone back to your sister now," Nikol said with a shrug. "I could have killed her, but I didn't, so you should be thanking me for that."

I was shaking in disbelief.

"Nikol, if you ever lay a hand on her again, I swear I'll be right at your throat in a minute," I growled. Nikol's face shifted into the most deadly expression I had ever seen. She pried my hands off her and stood up to look at my face.

"How could you stop loving me, Anastasia?" She said. "You used to love me so much."

"Nikol, you've changed."

"I did it because I love you!" she screamed back. "I wanted to be with you forever."

"No, you didn't love me," I said. "You love yourself. You love the idea of immortality. You've changed long before Alex did that for you. It's all because of your own greed!"

Nikol's eyes became dark and dangerous as she stared at me. She was gritting her teeth in pure rage. She knew whatever I sad was true, and she couldn't deny it.

Then she picked up the little white rabbit by its ears. The creature's tiny limbs thrust in her grip.

"You know what happens when I don't get my way?" she said. "If you and that girl ever get close to each other again..." she flashed her sharp teeth and bit into the white animal in the neck. The bunny twisted its body in pain. It was torturing just to watch. A minute later, Nikol drained the creature out of blood and dropped it on the floor like a piece of trash.

"Now you get the message," she said, wiping her blood-stained lips with the back of her hand. I felt helpless. Avery's safety was being threatened. I couldn't live with myself if anything like that happened to her. She was all I ever cared the most. I had never felt like that in my entire existence.

But if I didn't take Nikol back, Avery would be in serious dangers.

I stared at the little white ball on the floor and tried not to think of the worst in my head. Then Nikol came forward and ran her hand through my hair, her other hand played with the collar of my shirt. She gazed at me with an air of seduction radiated from her skin. I hated it. She brought her face closer to mine. I felt her lips tracing my jawline and over my cheeks.

"Let's bring back the old memories, shall we?" she whispered and pushed me down to the bed. She got on top of me and started pressing her lips to mine. I tried not to kiss her back, but it was impossible with her persistence.

I hated myself for doing this with her, but I had no choice.

Less than a minute, Nikol had ripped off my clothes, lifted one of my legs up to her waist as she ground her hips on me. She licked my throat and found her way into my mouth. Her tongue was soft and hot. It twisted and slithered hungrily against mine. All the while she kept moving against me and feeling my breasts.

I couldn't help feeling aroused under her sexual spell.

"I just want to taste those sweet lips again," she whispered in my ear. Then she went down and just like that I melted into her lust once again.

CHAPTER 16

AVERY

It was raining outside. The shadow of a willow tree danced on the creamy white walls of the room. Cold winds seeped through the window as I lay on the grand bed.

Since I was brought into this seeming paradise, I had never felt this miserable. I couldn't believe I had done it. I couldn't believe I even enjoyed doing it with Alex.

I was mad at her, but I was mad at myself more.

My entire beating heart was given to someone I loved, and yet here I was, sleeping with someone I hated. Then I felt a stir on the bed and the same fragrant smell of her skin came over me. Her soft silken hair brushed over my bare shoulder.

"Are you crying?" she said in the softest tone I had ever heard from her. It surprised me, and I didn't even know I was crying until then. I wiped the tears off my face but still kept my back turned to her. Her cold strong hand slid around my waist and pulled my body into hers.

"Don't cry," Alex said. "I'm sorry."

Her words drew me back to my senses. I turned around to face her. I didn't even know if I heard it right. Alexandra Romanov, the ruthless mistress of this house just said she was sorry to me.

"Oh now you're sorry?" I spat back in disgust. "Sorry for what? For violating me?"

She flinched. Then her expression changed back to the old sarcastic evil Alex. A slight smirk appeared on the corners of her perfect lips.

"Some of the time, yes, but most of the time, no," she said. "You enjoyed it with me, didn't you?"

I felt my cheeks burned with embarrassment. My mouth opened and closed but nothing came out. I turned my back to her again, yet she still kept a hold on me.

"Let go of me!" I said and tried to brush her hands off. With a swift motion, she pulled my body over, and I found myself lying on top of her.

I gasped.

Her hands locked around my waist. I couldn't move from her iron grip.

"Alex! What are you...*ughh!*" I groaned. She giggled back. I was still naked under the blanket. My face flushed hot.

"Come on, stop acting like you don't want me anymore," she said.

"Because I really don't!" I snapped back.

"Oh, sure." She arched a perfectly curved eyebrow in amusement. The golden shade of her eyes dimmed darker. I tried to look away, but I couldn't. It was like looking at the full moon, glorious and enchanting.

Her long black lashes fluttered over those dilated golden purples, which lit up even more with a deep glow. They were so mesmerizing. I traced my gaze over her narrow nose and then to her beautiful luscious lips, nothing but perfection could be described of her countenance. I was so lost in a trance-like state that Alex had to clear her throat.

"If you want to kiss me, go ahead, I don't mind." She grinned, showing off a set of flawless teeth. I jerked back from my daze and tried to get off her again, but Alex wouldn't let go. Instead, she reached one of her hands to the back of my neck and pulled my head down until our lips met.

Butterflies swooned inside my stomach. My skin prickled from the chill of her skin. But I found her lips moving over mine so tenderly and sweetly, a weird feeling began to form inside my core. My heart skipped and raced at the same time. Before I knew it, I found myself kissing her back, softly and slowly. My body seemed to have a life of its own. I didn't know what had gotten into me, but I kissed Alexandra back.

Her hands wandered down the sides of my body and pulled my knees up so that I was straddling her. She squeezed my backside as I faintly rocked back and forth. I knew it was wrong, but it felt strangely good with Alex. She kissed me with twirling, probing tongue. I used to hate the way her tongue always stuck inside my mouth, but now I let it roam freely.

Alex was a surprisingly great kisser. The way she turned her head and moved her lips was like poetry. It started to burn me inside.

Suddenly, I heard a low growl from the depth of her stomach. I broke the kiss, making a popping sound as I parted my lips from hers. Alex smiled sheepishly.

"Sorry," she said with a sheepish smile. "You're just making me hungry again."

I didn't know why it hurt to hear that, and why I even bothered to feel hurt now. I was nothing but a mere slave to her indulgence. I was just a slave to everyone. How could I be so stupid to fall for her charm and lost myself to lust?

Tears threatened to well up in my eyes, but I fought them back. I hated myself enough already. Why should I care about my so-called human dignity anymore?

"Fine," I said in a low quivering voice and brushed my hair to the side, baring the veins on my neck for her. Alex smiled and licked her lips.

"Come closer," she whispered. I leaned forwards and felt her cold breath on my skin. I shivered a little. Eyes closed, I braced myself for the pain, but instead of the burning sting, all I felt was a soft sweet kiss on my skin.

I jerked back and sat upright, staring at Alex in confusion.

"What was that for?" I said.

"What? I like you," she said with a shrug.

"Oh no, you don't," I said and quickly got off her. I grabbed my red dress and shrugged it on then hurried out of bed. "This can't be happening."

"Avery, wait!" Alex called out as I turned to the door.

But in a blinding flash, Alexandra was right in front of me. A desperate look marred on her face. It was the first time I saw her looking like that, but I pushed her away and tried to dodge around her. She was really fast, and before I could get to the door, Alex grabbed my body from behind and wrapped her strong arms around me.

Her narrow chin rested on my shoulder.

"Please, don't go," she said in a small voice that made me freeze, "Just give me a chance."

CHAPTER 17

I was back to my room in a daze. I didn't know what had just gotten into me or Alex. She had always been treating me worse than any other slaves in this house, but all of a sudden, she seemed like a different person. This was too much for my current state of mind. I got a splitting headache overanalyzing everything.

The next day, Alex wanted me downstairs first thing in the morning. I had to get dressed, but all I really needed was to be left alone in my room. Alex also insisted I move to her chamber. It took me a long time to protest the idea.

Finally convinced that I wouldn't run away, she let me have my way. Even if I could escape, where would I go now? I had no one as my refuge anymore, and I still couldn't stop thinking of Anastasia. Where was she at this moment?

But my mind must have been so messed up that every time I thought about her, Nikol's evil smile would also appear. Why didn't Ana tell me she already had a lover?

I just felt sick to the stomach.

"Miss. Pierce," a woman's voice came from outside my door. "My lady is waiting for you. Please be hurried."

It felt kind of weird being addressed properly for the first time.

"I'll be there in a minute," I said.

After I finished showering, I went to my closet, but all my old clothes were gone. The outfits I found inside were different. There were no more maid dresses. They all looked like expensive clothes. Each was tailored to perfection.

There were flowing silk laces, long gowns, lovely skirts and elegant scarves. There were beautiful embroidered dresses and all the fancy accessories you could imagine. Most of them had very intricate and classic designs.

"You've got to be kidding me," I muttered to myself, staring at those expensive items in disbelief. I had to spend a long frustrating moment to find the simplest things to wear, but it was still annoying being a flowing brown wool shirt and white shorts. I had to wrap a scarf around my wide collar. Maybe it was good for me not to expose too much of my skin around Alex.

I got downstairs and found Alex sitting elegantly on the table. A small basket placed beside her. But when she looked at me, she did this unexpected thing; Alexandra froze—she looked as if she just saw me for the first time.

Then she smiled. It was the most angelic smile I'd ever seen from her. She quickly floated to my side and wrapped her arms around my waist. There were other maids and bodyguards standing by the corners.

"Please, don't do that," I said, but Alex didn't seem to notice the on-lookers. She was just, well, being Alex.

"We should have a picnic together," She said breezily. I had never seen her being in such a good mood.

"A picnic?" I asked.

"Yes." Alex nodded and turned to the basket on the table. "I personally prepared something sweet and delicious to cheer you up."

"But why..."

"Come with me," she simply said and pulled me along.

Alex didn't answer anything I asked after that. And we walked until we were out of the grand garden of the mansion and then into the wooded area nearby.

I had never explored her estate before. It was too big, so I never knew the outside view would be so breathtaking.

There were hillsides and aspen trees, stretching far and wide.

Alex still kept holding my hand as we strolled together, and the strangest thing was I didn't try to pull away. We just walked like that in silence, going past the beautiful flowery bushes and water fountains. I could smell the scent of roses and dry leaves from a distance. It had been a long time since I saw such a dazzling view of the outside world.

The moment delighted me so much that when I looked at Alex again, I forgot about my sudden love crisis and smiled at her. She seemed a bit taken aback by that but she returned the smile quickly. Her golden pupils brightened even more. I never noticed how light they were under the sun.

My head snapped to her again.

"Alex!" I gasped.

"What is it?" she said, looking at me with questioning eyes.

"You can walk in the sun?"

Just like that, Alex burst out laughing.

"What? You think I should've burst into dramatic flames by now?" she said, shaking her head in amusement.

"Well, isn't it supposed to be a serious problem for—you know—vampires?" I said.

"Sort of," she said with a smirk. "But not for me. I'm special."

"I see." I nodded. "You're a high-class and oh-so-wow vampire."

Alex laughed again. It was weird hearing her laugh without being scared. Normally, all her laughter was always accompanied by her sarcastic, cold-hearted cruelty.

Now it was different.

"I like the way you talk, Avery. You really are something," she said and pinched my cheek hard. I swatted her hand away and shot her an annoyed look, but she just grinned mischievously at me.

A moment later, we came to the outskirt of the estate. Then I had to gasp at the sight in front of us. There was a beautiful archway with evergreen ivy hanging over it. White roses popped out from every angle of the trellises. It looked like those kinds of archways from a fairy tale. There were white roses everywhere.

Alex smiled at my reaction. She stepped forward and held her hand out to me.

"Will you come with me and be my rose princess?" she said.

I looked at Alexandra.

And without a straw of consciousness, I took her hand.

CHAPTER 18

We walked through the archway together. I kept glancing around the area. At the other side, I found the most beautiful garden anyone could ever imagine. Every corner of the earth was carpeted with green grass and clusters of white rose bushes. My nose constantly caught the fulfilling smell of sweet fragrance. Magnolias and forsythias bloomed like a sunny harbinger of spring. There were pink and purples flowers hanging from the tree branches. In this strange new world, everything looked freshly alien and beautiful.

"This place is a delight," I sighed in happiness.

"I know," Alex said. "I built it."

"You did?"

She just smiled.

Everything seemed alive in this place. Dry twigs cracked beneath our feet. There was a big pond not far away. The water was so clear, it mirrored the cloudless sky. I could see animals scuttling in search of food, some twittering, and some hiding. This was a living wood.

Alex walked me towards a big willow tree and started spreading the picnic mat on the grass. I watched her work, and it was sort of amusing because she looked like she had never done a thing in her life. I didn't know someone so graceful could be so awkward doing such mundane things.

I decided to help her. After we were done, we sat down together. She started preparing plates of cakes and cookies over the mat. I tried to focus my mind on other things while she prepared our tea. But my attention was soon drawn to the beautiful gourmet dessert she'd brought.

They were delicate and frosty and sweetly delicious.

Alex held a piece of strawberry mousse cake to me. I was hesitant but she insisted. She put it in my mouth, and I had never tasted anything like this for a very long time.

"Oh gosh, the cakes are so good. I think I'm going to have diabetes after this," I blurted before I could stop my human silliness. Alex laughed again.

She seemed really charming when she was like that. Was this a vampire lure they always talked about?

"Alex," I said while she was nibbling on some raspberry, "How did you become what you are now? How did you turn into a vampire?"

She looked at me. Then she took a sip of her tea and put the cup down and sighed.

"Alright, I'll tell you something about us, but don't press on it, alright?"

I nodded and waited for her to continue.

"I was born in 1899 into the House of Holstein-Gottorp Romanov," she said. "You know what it is, don't you?"

"Yes, the second and last dynasty that ruled the Russian Empire," I said, feeling proud of my history lesson back in the day. Alex nodded while stirring her tea with a silver-crested spoon.

"Czar Nicolas II was my father," she went on without looking at me. "My mother Czarina of Russia was also named Alexandra. She was a granddaughter of Queen Victoria of England. I always remember my mother as a beautiful woman, but not much of my father."

Alex smiled as if she was lost in the memories, and I could see a slight trace of sadness in her golden eyes. As promised, I didn't press on it.

"They had four daughters, including me," she added. "Anastasia was the youngest of the sisters. She was born in 1901. Then my brother Alexei came along."

"And where are they now?" I said.

"Oh, you think they're still alive?" Alex chuckled without humor. She looked up at me and then turned away. "They were all dead."

"But...but how could you...?"

"Only Anastasia and I survived the execution on July 17th." She shrugged as if it was normal. "With the help of a gunman and an Orthodox priest, we escaped death, and now we both are forever nineteen and seventeen. Isn't it great?"

But there was a sarcastic bitterness in her voice. I realized Alexandra wasn't always a blood-drinking enthusiast as I had always thought. There was something she didn't like about herself too.

"I woke up in a church besides Anastasia," she said. "Have you ever wondered why every royal family has to associate themselves with a religion or some sort of cult?"

"I don't know." I shook my head.

"Well," Alex said, "Just so you know, there is a reason behind it. How could a small group of people rule over hundreds of millions, not to mention for thousands of years? The secret of the royal lineage is that we had the Council consists of the top thirteen most influential families on Earth. Most people were unaware that the Earth's population was controlled by an "elite"— the Royal Council. And nobody on Earth could earn this membership. Either you are born into it or you are not."

"And you're one of them?"

"As you can see what happened after the war, most of the old royalties are back to rule their former empires. Europe is now ruled by the House of Hanover, the House of Hapsburg, and the House of Bernadotte. Royalties feel entitled to rule the world. It's been that way since the beginning of time if you haven't noticed. They believe they were the direct descendants of the superior race. Think about it. If they were just normal humans, what gave them the power to control others?"

I had no clue to how to respond to any of that.

"Let's get back to when you woke up," I changed the subject before I got another wave of a headache. "What happened to you after the rescue?"

"I was shot by the communist soldiers, along with my family, but I and Anastasia were not dead yet," she said. "The gunman dug us up from our graves and the priest helped us."

"Helped you— how?"

"I don't know. I'm not a priest!" she said with a shrug. "Maybe he dragged my soul back from hell or something. But when I woke up, I felt different— not quite human."

"Was the priest a vampire who changed you?"

"No, he was just an ordinary old man," she said. "I don't remember what he did, but I'm glad he didn't make Frankenstein's monsters out of us."

I choked on my tea. Alex laughed.

"So that means you just turned all by yourselves?" I said in amazement. "How could it be possible?"

"It's not easy as you think. There are many theories about us being vampires. You can look in the Bible the stuff about improper burial? Or you can find it in biology books about mutated genetics?"

"Oh, I see," I said. "It could be your genes. You're a royal. Your bloodline was so close to the higher power and all that, and those who died a violent death—"

"Enough of that, you're spoiling my picnic." Alex waved her hand off. I took it as a cue to stop talking. We continued having our tea in silence, but I still kept thinking about what she had just told me.

"So you both are the Last Grand Duchesses of Russia?" I couldn't help asking again.

"Aw, someone knows the history," Alex said. "Yes, we are."

"But I had seen the pictures of the four duchesses in the art gallery before," I said. "They looked different, not like you or Anastasia now. And I remember there wasn't anyone named Alexandra among them."

"You are quite observant." Alex said. "Well, humans grow old and die, but vampires are different. They can't age or die, so they keep changing and evolving. The older we get, the better we look—and stronger, too. Now, you can say, I'm a very hot and sexy a-hundred-and-thirteen-year-old woman. Aren't you jealous?"

"Very," I said and rolled my eyes at her. "But how about the name?"

"After I was reborn, the priest named me after my mother," Alex said casually. "My former name is Marie Nikolevna Romanova."

CHAPTER 19

ALEXANDRA

It felt strange finding myself talking so much and so easily with her. It was like the girl had a key to unlock all my past, and she did it without me realizing it. For the first time, my memories didn't feel like as sharp pain in my chest anymore. It was just some distant finished events.

I felt so free and so alive, like a caterpillar turning into a butterfly.

Avery kept staring at me with her jaw hanging.

"When are you going to close your mouth, Avery?" I said to her. She snapped back to herself again and blinked her eyes.

"Alex, there's something else I want to ask you, too," Avery said in a hesitant voice. She couldn't even look at me.

"About Nikol, right?" I said. Avery looked up with a surprised face and then she nodded sheepishly.

"What do you want to know?" I asked.

"Everything," she whispered, staring straight into my eyes. I looked away. I didn't know why it was so hard to breathe when I knew she still cared about my sister. I wanted her to be with me and only me. Suddenly I found myself terribly afraid of losing her.

But I tried to understand. It would take sometimes. By then I would make her mine, forever.

I exhaled before starting.

"Nikol was the daughter of a Bolshevik general, the communist officer," I said. "She took us in when we had no home."

"And how did she and... Ana...you know...get together?" Avery asked. I tried to ignore a rising twinge in my chest when I knew she still cared about my sister.

"Anastasia was still young back then. She needed someone to comfort her," I said. "Obviously, I wasn't a good sister to do that, so Nikol took care of everything. She would give her blood to Anastasia, and just like everyone else, they fell in love."

Avery winced at the last sentence. This must have hurt her so much, and seeing them back together was a real torment. I knew that feeling. I'd been through it myself.

"So that was when Nikol was still human?"

"Yes, once upon a time," I said. "But after a while, she decided that she wanted to live with my sister forever, so I fulfilled her wish."

"You mean you turned her into a vampire?" Avery cried in surprise.

"What? I was just helping them." I shrugged. "But my silly sister didn't even thank me for that."

"If I were Anastasia, I would get very mad too. No wonder why you and your sister don't get along," she said, frowning at me in accusation.

"Good, now you know."

"And what happened to them after that? Why didn't I see Nikol earlier?"

"Oh since then that two have always been off and on for decades," I told her and snickered to myself, "I didn't get what the fuss Ana was in. It was like all hell broke loose every time they were together too long. Then Anastasia followed me here because I had to move here to avoid their annoying fighting and love-making. What a pain!"

Avery's big brown eyes glared at me. I knew hearing bad stuff about Anastasia really bothered her, but I didn't even feel sorry in this case.

"Should I continue?" I said later.

"No thank you, I think I've heard enough," she said.

"Alright then." I nodded, I was glad to get off the hook at last. When I took another sip of my tea, Avery turned to me again.

"And how about you?" she said. "Have you ever fallen in love with anyone?"

I almost spurted the drink out of my mouth. I looked at the girl in front of me again. No one had ever asked me that. And no one had ever come so close to my heart like she had. Her humanity irritated me, her stubbornness drove me crazy, but above all, she made me feel. All my emotions came back, and it was annoying, but I almost felt like I was alive again.

"Hmm?" Avery leaned her face forward, waiting for an answer.

"You've got cream on your lip," I said.

"Oh, where?" she said, trying to wipe it off.

"Let me."

I moved closer to her, our shoulders almost touched. I reached my finger to wipe the white cream from her pink lips, and then put it into my mouth. Our eyes met. And as we looked into each other's eyes, I could feel the electric sparks in the air. I put my hand back to her cheek, slipping a finger slowly into her mouth and played with her velvety tongue. She closed her soft moist lips around it and sucked it, which made my heart pump wildly. Then I stroked her face with my hand, tracing the outline of her curved lips with my thumb. She sighed softly.

"You're doing it again, aren't you?" Avery asked.

"Doing what?" I said.

"Seduce me."

"No, I'm not seducing you," I told her. "I'm doing what my heart tells me to."

Avery's eyes looked up through her long lashes and blushed.

"I don't know what I should think of you Alex," she whispered. "It's so confusing right now."

"Then don't think," I said and brought my lips close to hers, "Just feel."

And I kissed the corner of her mouth lightly and sat back. I could see the effect I had left on her skin. She wanted me as much as I wanted her. I could see her temptation building up. This was a human need.

"Come here," I said.

Avery bit her bottom lip, but then she did move toward me. I welcomed her into my arms and made her straddle on my lap. Our faces were extremely close. I looked into her beautiful brown eyes and smiled. Her cheeks blushed brightly. I stroked her small back under her shirt. She gingerly put her arms around my neck.

Her eyes lingered on my face with hidden emotions.

"Alex, tell me why you were so horrible to me at the beginning," she began in a soft voice, "and all of a sudden, you're doing this with me?"

I sighed and rested my head on her chest. I hugged her delicate body in my arms and didn't want to let go. Her hand smoothed my hair gently as I breathed in her sweet smell. I closed my eyes and listened to her heartbeats.

"Do you know how many years I had stopped smelling the scent of the flowers, and all the trees of the forest had stopped looking green to me? Because the moment I saw you," I said, feeling my throat tightened, "All those years faded away. Finally, I'm able to wake up feeling the anticipation to be with someone. I also knew you could hurt me worse than anyone ever could. And I had to hurt you first, because when I first saw you, I never would have imagined such a strong burning desire. I just didn't know I was already in love. I don't know what you have done to me, but I want you so much, it hurts."

I had no idea where it came from, but all the words just flowed from my mouth like running river. Avery let me hold her like that without saying anything. Then when I looked at her again, she brought her palms to my cheeks and kissed my forehead. When her lips parted, I pulled her down for a kiss on my lips and deepened it. She was a bit hesitated, but I tightened my arms around her body. And slowly, she seemed to let go of the tension.

Her hands run through my hair as I pulled her hips against mine. The heat radiating from her body excited me again.

Slowly I pulled her shirt over her head and unhooked her bra. Avery didn't stop me anymore. I buried my face in her soft round breasts, inhaling the wonderful scent. And as my mouth wrapped around her nipples, I felt them become erect against my tongue. She gasped in my ear even I knew she had tried to hide the sound like she was trying to smother it, but I still heard her. I fell back on the mat, taking her with me. I traced my mouth back to hers again. Her lips moved faster and deeper against mine. I unzipped her shorts and slipped it down, letting her naked body pushed into me.

Avery took a short break to pull my knitted blazer and unbuttoned my shirt. Then I rolled her off and got on top of her. She was breathing hard as I kept kissing her everywhere. Her fingernails dug into my back with her legs wrapped around my waist. I started moving my hips. I was grinding so hard it made her muscles clench, her jaw dropped in ecstasy, and her hands clung tighter. I cupped her firm breasts as I kept moving. She spread her legs wider as if she wanted to suck me in. Then I slipped my hand down. Avery squeezed her eyes shut; devouring the worldly pleasure I was giving her. She bit her lips trying not to moan, but my fingers teased her until she gave up.

"Oh Alex!" she said between gasps and whimpers.

"Much obliged, my rose princess," I whispered, and I licked my way down her breasts and to her flat stomach, and then ended up between her thighs. I felt my fingers slip inside her as my tongue twisted over her sensitive rosebud. I had never wanted to please anyone like this before. Her overwhelming joy was so palpable; I could feel it enveloping me, making me moan along with her.

I slid my fingers slowly into her wet opening. My tongue curled mercilessly on her tiny pink pearl. I started thrusting down her slippery gate. After a short while, when I could tell she was about to come, I stopped the motion, causing her to wince desperately. For some wicked reason, I still enjoyed torturing her with my cruel sense of love. Avery clenched her teeth as I began stroking even deeper, harder, and faster until her muscles shook, her hips raised from the ground. I could hear her pulse beating frantically with screaming joy.

Less than a second, I brought her back to the edge of orgasm, but once again when she was about to reach her climax, I slowed down. The girl almost cursed me. I felt pity for her, but I didn't want to let her off yet. Avery was so hot; her eyes were unfocused with too much sensual pleasure. I was saving the best thing last. Without breaking the rhythm, I lifted one of her legs and hung it over my shoulder. Her eyes widen as I concentrated on the weakest, deepest spot inside her heaven. The juicy nectar dripped through my fingers.

Until once again, she couldn't stop herself, the moment had come. Avery gave into a screaming orgasm. Her voice echoed into the wood. Her hands clutched the mat as her body cum and twisted in uncontrollable pleasure.

She panted, trying to catch her breathe. Like always, I slowly slipped my fingers out and licked them. Then I hovered over her body to check if my love was back from the moon yet.

"Are you alright, sweetheart?" I smoothed her hair gently. Avery didn't face me, but she was panting with a dazed look.

"I hate you, Alex," she said in a weak voice, her body was still shuddering under me.

"I know." I smiled and comforted her with light kisses on her cheek.

CHAPTER 20

AVERY

It was already dark when we walked back to the mansion. Alex put her arm around my shoulders all the way. The grass of the garden was damp and slippery from the night dew. I would have fallen on my face if she hadn't held me.

Alex could see far better than me in the dark. Her extraordinary night vision made her eyes glow slightly. And instead of looking scary, I found that very fascinating.

"What?" Alex said when she caught me peering at her for the fourth time.

"Nothing," I replied.

"We'll be there sooner if you just concentrate on walking," she said and shook her head at me. Alex might be a little grumpy at times, but deep down; I knew her meanness was just a mask she put on. When we got out of the garden, she held my hand firmly, still refusing to let go. I looked down at our joined hands. With Anastasia, I was always the one who cared more and worried more. I was worried that she wouldn't like me as much, which turned out to be true. I was constantly afraid of losing her every second, even when I was with her.

I still felt like I wasn't good enough and didn't deserve her love. Besides Ana belonged to someone else— someone better and more beautiful like Nikol.

I pinched the bright of my nose and winced at the thought.

"What's wrong, Avery? Are you alright?" Alex stopped on her track and turned to look at me in concerns.

"Nothing," I lied. "I'm just a little tired."

"Stop saying that one word already," she scolded. "I can take you there faster if you're not feeling well."

"I think I'll throw up on you if you get me there in your crazy vampire speed," I told her.

Alex thought it over then she shrugged.

"Well, my clothes are too expensive for that," she said at last, and I couldn't help giggling a little.

We came closer to the mansion.

As we walked by the marble fountain, Alex suddenly paced a step ahead and turned around to face me. The scent of her flawless skin brushed against my nose. It was something wonderful than any perfume I had any memory of. But what surprised me was her angelic face close to mine.

But what made me blink in confusion was that Alex just grabbed my face and kissed me. The kiss was long and passionate as if she wanted to engrave some spells on my lips. And then she broke away, leaving me breathless.

"Thanks for today." She smiled. I was about to smile back when I caught a glimpse of someone standing by the main door. The familiar goddess figure stood motionlessly under the hall light.

Anastasia stared at us. I didn't know how long she had been here, or what she had witnessed, but the look in her eyes was the most painful thing I had ever seen. I was sure my heart dropped somewhere near my ankle as I looked back at her. Anastasia was here. Finally, she wasn't just my beautiful dream that got shuttered. For the past few days, I tried to pretend that I had forgotten about that dream, but now she was back. It made everything seem more surreal and more unbearable again.

Alex turned back around and reached for my hand. She squeezed it gently.

"Oh, you're back, little sister," she said with a slight smirk on her face.

"So it seems," Anastasia replied in a flat tone.

"Sorry, we didn't welcome you properly. We were busy having a picnic and a little fun time together, right Avery?"

For a moment, I just wanted to crawl into a hole and never get out again. I couldn't look at Ana now. She said nothing, but I could feel her eyes fixed on me. Alex must have seen her sister and knew that she was there watching us.

Then another girl came into sight. I recognized her without a doubt. She came and looped her hand around Ana's arm possessively. The perfect brown hair spiraled down her slender body. Her violet eyes sparkled like dancing stars, but when she turned her face to me, it felt like a stab in my stomach. I almost heaved the picnic food out.

I looked down on my shoes and tried not to let my knees buckle. Then Alex pulled me by the hand. And as we walked toward them, the world seemed to slow down to a crawl. I couldn't tell if Anastasia were having a hard time seeing me again. She didn't glance at my direction or break herself away from Nikol. It didn't take long to know what hurt me the most, losing someone you love or being replaced by someone else. I definitely hated both.

Nikol flashed a poisonous smile at me when we entered the hallway. I lowered my face to avoid her eye contact.

"Nice to see you again, Nikol," Alex said.

"You too."

"How about a dinner together?"

I felt Alex's hand slid around my waist. Anastasia stared straight at her sister. I had never seen Ana's eyes so piercing cold like that. For some reason, I knew she also refused to look at me.

"Sounds great," Nikol said sweetly. "We have a lot to catch up anyway."

"Good, see you at the table then." Alex waved her hand, and finally, we were able to walk away after ten or twelve years later, for it did feel that long to me.

CHAPTER 21

Dinner in a house full of royal vampires was no different than any normal family's dinner, except the food consisted of red juicy meat and blood. The feast itself was enough to feed an entire village. I had never seen so much food like this ever since the war ended.

My seat was next to Alex's. She was sipping her red wine at the head of the table.

At last, Anastasia came down and took a seat opposite me. I was relieved that a whole roasted pig with an apple stuck in its mouth provided me enough coverage. I didn't want to face her.

We heard the sound of high-heels echoed sharply from the hall. Nikol floated into view, but I kept my eyes glued to my plate as she walked to us. Nikol was wearing a long flowing white dress with a neck so low, she reminded me of a character from the Greek mythology.

"Oh, what a nice banquet, Alex," she said merrily. Before Nikol took a seat, she turned to cup Anastasia's chin in her hand and turned her face to hers before kissing her in front of me. A piece of sesame bread suddenly turned to ash in my mouth.

"Get a room," Alex said as she put her wine glass down on the table.

Ana looked a bit startled, but she didn't say anything.

"We already did." Nikol flashed a perfect smile back and sat down beside Ana.

"So," Alex exhaled and rested her elbows on the table and laced her fingers together. "Any news from Moscow?"

"Nah, same old, same old." Nikol shrugged, stabbing her beef steak with a silver fork. "I should have moved here sooner. It was boring without you there."

"Oh, so you want to stay here, too?" Alex said. "I didn't expect you and my sister to get back together so quick."

"Don't exaggerate, Alex," Anastasia spoke up. "It's been twelve years."

I lifted my eyes from the plate. For a brief second, I felt like she wanted me to know they hadn't been together for a long time. They had been broken up for twelve years. I was just five back then. I noticed Ana wasn't eating. She was pushing her food around the plate. A grim expression seemed to be permanent on her face.

"Never mind, though," Nikol said with a smile. "I know we will always get back together eventually." She put her hand on Ana's and stroked it flirtingly. Then she turned and smiled right at me. I quickly dropped my eyes to avoid her eyes, but my lungs seemed to work harder than usual just to breathe.

We started eating in silence.

"Anyway, I'm a bit amazed that you allow a human to sit at the same table with us," Nikol suddenly said again.

I desperately hoped my face wouldn't flush so hard. Anastasia's face twitched as if someone jabbed her with a needle.

"As far as I remember you were once a human, too, Nikol," Alex said, turning to stare at her. Nikol made a pouty face. If I wasn't mistaken, Alexandra was defending me. "Besides, I'm positive Avery's not going to be the same forever."

I didn't understand what she meant for the last part, but Anastasia's head snapped right up at Alex. She looked at her squarely in the eyes. I could feel the tension began to stir in the air.

"What do you mean by that, Alex?" she asked through her clenched teeth.

"Oh you know very well what I mean, sister," Alex replied, twirling the wine around in her crystal glass. "Avery is going to stay with me for a long, long time, and you know that, don't you?"

"You can't do this, Alexandra!" Anastasia dropped her fist on the table with a loud bang. I jumped up along with the roasted pig.

"I don't see why not," Alex said, looking back at her sister.

The two of them stared at each other with an equal amount of force. Nikol shot a sharp look at me as if I was the cause of it all. And I kind of was, considering the fact that they were talking about me.

"I will not let you do that," Anastasia growled.

"It's none of your business," Alex said. "You better take care of your personal matter now, little sister."

Anastasia gritted her teeth, but she still couldn't overwhelm Alex. Then with an angry hiss, she stormed out of the dining hall. Nikol threw her napkin on the table with a bored face and stood up.

"Well, thanks a lot for the dinner, Alex," she said.

"You're welcome."

And then she too was out of there. I turned to Alexandra, who simply continued eating like nothing happened. I knew better than to say anything at that moment. I wasn't stupid. The whole conversation was about me and my future doom. And I got a feeling that it was something I had no control of.

Chapter 22

ANASTASIA

I walked into my room and I felt like I wanted to tear down everything in sight. Alex just couldn't do that again. Not to Avery. I was always the one to clean up the mess she left behind. Nikol was a good example of it. Now Avery was going to be her next victim. How could she be so heartless and ignorant?

Nikol appeared. She stood by the door with her arms crossed.

"You do care about that human girl, don't you?" she said. I didn't want to answer her. I didn't want to talk to anyone. All I could think of was Avery. I had come back worried sick about her, wondering how Alex had been treating her in my absence.

But things turned out funny at the end. It wasn't Avery who got tortured. It was me. Alex finally found a way to rip my heart out alive. She stole Avery from me and threatened to turn her. My head was on the verge of exploding thinking about it. I walked to the table and poured myself a glass of whiskey. Then I slammed myself down on the couch. Nikol came to my side as I downed the burning liquid in one gulp. I just needed to distract myself from this madness. When I reached for the bottle again, Nikol grabbed my hand.

"You know, you're making me jealous when you do that," she said.

"Nikol, just don't start," I said, trying not to sound as annoyed as I already was.

"You leave me no choice, Anastasia," she said, bringing her palm to my face. "And you also know, I'm not good at controlling my jealousy. You have been warned."

"Nic..." I started again, but she took the empty glass from my hand and put it down on the table. Then she pushed me back against the couch. Nikol leaned over me. Her seductive face was close to mine. And something about the look in her violet eyes made me stay still. I had forgotten that I was a prisoner of someone else.

My thought went back to Avery. What had Alex done to her? I just didn't understand. When Alex kissed her, I thought every cell in my body was ready to burst into flames. I wanted to bolt out and rip Alex's tongue off for that.

The image of them kissing kept rolling back into my head.

"Tonight I forgive you for your misbehavior," Nikol said. "But I have to make sure you remember how concerned I am about your poor anger-management."

Nikol stood straight again and smoothly slipped her long white dress off her shoulders. The silk fabric fell to the floor without a sound.

"Nikol, I'm not in a mood," I told her, taking my eyes off her naked body.

"I can always make you," she came to whisper in my ear. Then she traced her crimson lips over my neck and all the way to my chest. I turned my face aside as her cold breath stung my skin. Nikol just gripped my chin and turned my head back to look at her and then she locked our lips. I secretly winced at the kiss. Her cherry-scented lips were too sweet for my liking. I felt Nikol's hands stroked my thighs.

"Spread your legs," she said.

"Don't talk like that to me," I retorted with a glare, but she didn't seem to care. Then she shoved her hand down my pants and pushed me back to the couch. I had to gasp as her long fingers started messing with my private place.

"You are so tense," Nikol breathed, "You need to loosen up a little."

And before I had time to even think, she stripped off my pants and parted my knees. I felt her hand keep fiddling over my sensitivity. Her fingers teased all over.

The sensation went from mildly annoying to highly erotic. My breath quickened as fast as my racing heartbeats. Then Nikol's face dove right down on me and wagged her tongue against my heated core. This was her favorite game. She would take away my sanity and made me surrender to her lust.

Nikol twirled her soft long tongue around the rim of my private. My head threw back as her long sleek tongue delved deep into me. I was in for a whole new world.

My legs began shaking. The mounting ecstasy made my jaw drop.

One of my hands tried to hold onto the couch while my other hand entangled in Nikol's hair. Maybe it was my sexual frustration that made me do this, but I couldn't help imagine Avery instead. I imagined her sweet warm lips on my skin.

My perfect fantasy was only real with that one girl, but before I could stop myself, I blurted her name out loud.

Suddenly, everything froze.

I just wanted to swallow the word back the way a frog catches a fly in mid-air, but Nikol already heard it. She paused and looked up at me with those blazing violet eyes. Then her face rose up to me in a flash. I knocked myself back against the couch. Nikol's lips pulled over her white sharp teeth.

"That's it, Anastasia!" Nikol snapped in my face. "What is it with that human slave anyway?"

"I'm sorry, Nikol," I shuttered. "I won't let it happen again. I promise."

"If you still want to keep her around, you better stop acting like this with me, you hear me?"

I winced and nodded obediently. Nikol could be so scary when she needed to. But it was all my fault. Avery's life was at stake because of me. I shouldn't have dragged her into all this. Nikol seemed to notice the nervous look in my eyes. She brought her hand to my cheek gently.

"Can't we just start it all over again, Anastasia?" She said.

I didn't know what to do. I had to agree with whatever she asked. There was no turning back now. I nodded.

Nikol came to kiss me again, and I forced myself to return the favor by kissing her back as passionately as I could. We both got up and like a whirlwind, we found ourselves collapsing on the bed together.

I had to endure it for Avery.

CHAPTER 23

In the time of a vampire apocalypse, I never thought I could survive as long as I did now. It was a hell on earth, but I had found a new kind of hell. It burned you from the inside out. It would have been better if I wasn't bought into the Romanov House.

Everything would be over quickly and less painful.

I felt like my life only existed in a glass box again. All things happened around me, but I had no control over any of it. As in the case of today, I opened my door to find Anastasia standing before me. My heart just stopped. I guess I was having a mini heart attack.

"Shhh…" she hushed, putting an index finger to her lips. She got inside and closed the door behind her. "Avery, I don't have much time."

"What? Anastasia, what are you…?" I started to say, but she just pulled me by my hand and dragged me into the bathroom. Her face was a mask. I couldn't tell what her intention was.

"What are you doing?" I asked, but she didn't answer and just closed the bathroom door again. Then she came over to open the water on the bathtub, letting the noisy flow engulf the silence around us.

I stood there dumbfounded. She turned around to look at me at last. Her deep golden eyes made every function in my body freeze. It was a mixture of hurt and anger. Just yesterday, she couldn't even bring herself to look at me. Now Anastasia was in my bathroom. I blinked at the seriousness on her angelic face. Without saying a word, Anastasia came up to me and pushed me against the wall. Her body pressed into mine. The next thing I knew, her tongue was already slithering inside my mouth. This unexpected intimacy surprised me. For some reason, I couldn't tell if she was doing it because she wanted me or she was just mad at me. Her furious kiss burned my skin.

"Ana, stop it!" I said, trying to push her away, but she wouldn't budge. Her hot lips went down my throat and over my chest.

"You hurt me, Avery," she said. "I couldn't stand seeing you with Alex."

I should have felt bad and embarrassed, but for that moment, all I could think of was how my heart ached for her touch. And slowly, I felt my body begin to melt into hers again. Anastasia turned us around and sat me on the edge of the sink. She lifted my thighs up and got between them, wandering her hands inside my skirt. Her lips ran over my jaw and down my throat, causing me to gasp elatedly. It was all I ever wanted to feel.

Her hands pulled my panties off and wrapped my legs around her waist. Everything happened so fast, my mind whirled. I didn't even realize when she got her pants off until the moment our skins merged together. Her hips started moving against me. Ana raised one of my legs up high and spread them wider. I leaned my body back, so I could be more accessible to her. I bit my lips, trying to hold my moans from this incredible feeling down there. It was like all that existed was our joined paradises. Our breath quickened as the slippery motion was driving us wild—until we couldn't contain it any longer, and we burst in electric delight. A flaming orgasm erupted between our legs. The sensation was too strong; I was hauled forward into Ana's arms. She caught me, and we gasped over each other's shoulder. After what seemed like a long time, we finally broke off. Ana gave a gentle kiss on my lips and helped me off the sink. My legs felt wobbly, but at least I could stand. We gathered our clothes again and Ana came to wrap her arms around me.

I looked at Anastasia's face, trying to remember the last time I felt so loved. I wanted her to know, I still loved her, I still loved her with all my heart and soul.

"I'm sorry, Avery, I'm so sorry," she said. "I miss you too much, I couldn't contain myself."

"Why? What happened?" I whispered. "You already have Nikol."

"I don't care about Nikol!"

"Then why?" I said again, staring into her deep golden eyes for the answer, "I don't understand."

Anastasia just turned her face away from me.

"Nikol threatens me," she said, looking as if she was ashamed of herself. "I'm sorry, but we can't be seen together. You can get hurt being with me."

"So you want to break up with me?" This question took every ounce of my gut to ask.

"No! Avery, I love you. Nikol means nothing to me, she's just my past."

"But she's your first."

"Avery, please," she held my face in her palms and looked into my eyes. "I don't care about anyone but you. Listen, you have to trust me. I will find a way to get us back together again. I promise. Just wait for me, alright?"

Anastasia brought her soft beautiful lips to my forehead. The kiss burned with anguish and longing on my skin, causing tears to spring from my eyes.

"I have to go," she whispered and then turned to the door. "Please take care."

In just a blink, Anastasia already left through the door, leaving me standing there with my empty chest.

CHAPTER 24

ANASTASIA

I reached Alex's office and waved the guards away. They bowed and left the hall. I didn't even bother to knock before I got in. Alex was sitting on her wide antique desk in front of a large window. Victor was standing beside her chair while she was reading some files. He bowed when he saw me, but Alex didn't even look up.

"What brought you here, sister?" she said with an expression of a brick wall.

"Alex, we need to talk," I told her.

"About what?"

I turned to Victor. Our eyes met, and he understood then left the room.

"I want to ask you for a favor."

"A favor? Wow, I'm flattered."

"It's about Nikol, Alex," I said. "Please, you have to get her back to Russia."

"Anastasia," she said as she finally looked up at me. "I don't have all day for this. If you want to talk about Nikol with me, you might as well talk to a tree."

"You think this is a game?" I sneered. "Nikol is in the house! And here you are, acting like there's nothing wrong with her."

Alex stood up and stared at me.

104

"And what does your girlfriend have to do with me?"

"She has everything to do with you, Alex," I said. "You created her. You're the only one who can make her listen."

"If you keep your distance from Avery, then there's nothing you should be worried about," she said.

"You still don't understand, do you? Nikol is like a walking time bomb," I said again. "It's just a matter of time until something snaps. And if anything ever happens to Avery, I will never forgive you."

"I can protect her," Alex simply said. "You stay the hell away from her, that's your job."

I clenched my jaw, feeling the throbbing pain in my gum. This conversation wasn't going to get anywhere. The least I could do was to beg, but I would never let Alexandra get that satisfaction from me. I stepped closer to my sister.

"You're afraid, aren't you?" I said. "You're afraid that I will take Avery back because you know you can't win over her heart. Avery is in love with me."

Alex's eyes blazed like burning embers. She gripped the edge of the table. I thought she was going to flip it over at me, but then she took a deep breath as if to calm down and then she smiled again.

"You should have seen her face when I made her come," she said.

At those words, I was ready to throw myself across the table at her, but someone knocked on the door. It took all my willpower not to tear Alex into shreds. I swallowed back the burning rage as Victor came in with an urgent look.

"My lady, there's an important letter from Kremlin," he said and handed a gold envelope to my sister. She tore it open and skimmed through the paper. A frown creased her smooth face.

"What is it?" I asked out of curiosity.

"The Royal Council asks for my return," she said.

"What happened?"

"It's the hunters. They're making quite a riot in Moscow," she said and dropped the letter on the table with a low sigh.

"Will you go back?" I asked.

"What? You think it will hand you a chance to be with Avery again?" Alex looked into my eyes. I had to admit I was counting on that.

"You think about it, Alex," I said. "But if you claim that you're the one for her, you should give her some space. Let Avery decide."

We held each other's gaze for a moment.

Then I turned and walked out of the room.

CHAPTER 25

The room was brighter than usual. There was a different chill to it too. It was quite welcoming in a way that I wanted to curl up into a ball and never leave. Then this rare thought surprised me. Why did I feel comfortable in Alexandra's chamber? I should be anxious or even scared.

Instead, all I harbored in my heart was this cozy calmness.

Alex had sent for me again this evening. Of course, I couldn't refuse her order.

Most of the curtains were now opened. I noticed the uplifting change after I walked into her room. I wandered further and found Alex sitting on the bench of her black piano. She looked like she was in some deep thoughts. When she heard me coming, Alex turned around and gave me a whole-hearted smile. That smile made my breath hitch in awe. Alex was so dazzling when she smiled.

"Come and sit here with me, my rose princess," she said, holding her hand out.

I walked up to her. I was about to sit down when Alex pulled me onto her lap instead. She wrapped her arms around my waist and stared up into my wide eyes. I couldn't help blushing away.

"You look so lovely when you blush," she said.

I turned my face to her again. At the same time, Alex leaned forward and stole a kiss on my lips. My cheeks reddened even more. She giggled melodiously at my reaction. I tried to bite my lips from smiling, but it felt so nice to hear her laugh.

"You want to listen to some music?" She asked to my surprise. And when I kept staring at her mutely, Alex released me from her hold again. I sat back down on the bench next to her as she opened the glossy piano lid. She placed her hands gently and gracefully on the keys. I had never noticed how long and beautiful her fingers were until then. I swear they sort of took my breath way.

Alex traced the tips of her slender fingers over the piano. I was still admiring how strikingly delicate her hands looked, when suddenly every thought was pushed out of my mind— blown away by the flowing melodies as Alex started playing.

The melodic notes were slow at first, but then it got more harmonious and full of vibrating pitches. The music seemed to flow from those delicate hands effortlessly. I sat there, paralyzed from the acoustic sensation that shook every cell in my being. Now, I understood why Anastasia said Alex was a genius. It seemed as if her music could make everything come to life with it. It had made her come alive as well. The animated song was lively and strong, sometimes with occasional humorous tones— just like Alexandra herself.

I looked sideway at her marvelous face. Her thick curved lashes were so long, they almost brushed her cheeks. A lovely smile curled at the corners of her luscious lips as she played. I couldn't picture the bitter Alex anymore. The one I was sitting with now was a total different person.

As Alex reached the end of the song, she held the final note longer than its full value and let the heavenly sounds vanish back into the air.

She exhaled and turned her face to me with a sheepish smile.

"Sorry, I felt a bit nervous playing for you," she said. "I haven't done it in a very long time."

"Alex, that was the most beautiful thing I've ever heard," I told her. "You're beautiful!"

She raised an eyebrow at me. Then I realized what I just said.

"Er...I referred to the music," I tried to correct myself. "The music was beautiful."

Alex laughed whole-heartedly. Then she put her arms around me again and pulled me back against her. She kissed my temple and let my head rest on her chest.

"I think I'm going to miss you like crazy, Avery," she said, smoothing my hair.

"Why did you say that?" I pulled away from her with a frown. "What's wrong?"

"I have to go back to Kremlin for a little while," she said. "The hunters are causing a stir there. Some loose ends to tie."

I knew a few things about the hunters. They were the only enemy of the vampire race— the only ones who dared to defy the new order. Their goal was to liberate humans from the vampire's oppression. Most of the hunters were trained to be skilled assassins. They would hide and attack whenever they got a chance.

For a moment, I didn't know how I should feel about this news. Alex kept studying my face as if to search for some sort of reactions from me. I had no idea how I looked to her, but she just leaned in to kiss the corner of my lips.

"Don't worry about me, I'll be back soon," she said. Our eyes lingered on each other's faces. I could see her golden pupils widened with pouring emotions. Then her lips curved up in a mischievous grin.

"But meanwhile we're still together, why don't we..."

"No...no..." I said, shaking my head vigorously before she could finish.

Alex flashed an alluring smile at me again, the kind of smile that could melt my bones. I knew that smile. And it was time to run, or else I would be so done.

I pried her hands off and got up, but Alex pulled my body back to hers quite easily. She laughed and started tickling me all over. I hated that, but I couldn't help twisting in laughter and half-heartedly yelled, "No!" and "Stop!", yet I wasn't even convincing to myself.

She finally stopped and then held me still.

"Just a little, please?" Alex whispered in my ear and nuzzled my neck earnestly. She traced her tongue over my goose-bumped skin. Her hands slithered inside my shirt from behind. They kept feeling every inch of my body. There was this lustful part of me that anticipated the things we had done— things that we shouldn't have done but would still do. I had tried to draw the line between submission and protest, but the line had been long gone, crossed and erased to nothingness. There was no way I could restrain myself from falling hard under the spell of Alexandra Romanov.

When the mood and the urge struck, I found myself surrendered completely to her. I had become a mindless prey at last— the kind of prey that I didn't realize I longed to be.

One of Alex's hands slid down between my parted thighs. Her long delicate fingers gave me a gentle, playful fondle over my already wetted part. My heart pounded. My adrenaline raced.

"Let's go to bed, shall we?" Alex whispered into my ear. I could barely nod, but deep down I knew what my answer would be.

CHAPTER 26

I was lying on Alex's bed again. My head spun with a shameless excitement. I pushed myself up to recollect my thoughts. But the sight of Alex undressing herself made my mind freeze and my breath catch in my throat. I stared at her stunning body in wonder and awe. She unbuttoned her silk blouse one at a time, revealing her firm breasts underneath her black lacy bras.

My body was lit up in prickled flames.

After Alex shed off all her outer layers, she moved over me like a graceful lioness. My pulse hammered in my ears. Then I let her unbutton my white shirt, unhooked my bras and slipped off my skirt. But she shredded away my panties, tearing it from my grasping thighs.

Alex pulled me by the legs and spread them wide. My heart pounded faster. I could see her eyes gleamed with needs as she stared at my nakedness. I should have felt embarrassed, but everything she did simply set my whole being aflame.

Alex lowered her elegant body over me. A burst of burning sensation ran through whole being once we touched skin to skin. In that moment, I learned the truth about myself— that I did love being taken by Alexandra Romanov.

"I'm falling in love with you each time I see you, Avery, you know that," she whispered as she hovered over me. "You don't have to love me back, but there's nothing you can do to change how I feel about you, ever."

I gazed back into her eyes. The same tingling feeling aroused from the pit of my stomach. When she leaned in and placed her lips against mine, I devoured her scented lips as earnestly as she did mine. Then her soft curling velvety tongue swirled inside my mouth. This sensual gentle touch made my mind twirl. My entire body was screaming.

Alex held my hands up above my head as she kissed and nibbled my lips. She ran her fingers along my jaw and nibbled on my neck and shoulders. I heard myself whimper as she sucked hard on my skin. Her hand stroked over my breasts and squeezed them, my back arched from the bed. I felt her hands scratch lightly on my sides as she licked and sucked on my hardened nipples. My hips kept moving upward against hers without even realizing it. It seemed to please Alex. She wrapped one of my legs over her waist and continued to kiss me. Suddenly, I felt the tips of her fingers made their way down to my purring hot pot. Just the touch of her hand sent me a jolt of electrifying ecstasy. I gasped, throwing my head back. And before I could recover from the first move, Alex, being mean in bed as she always was, slipped a finger inside my dripping softness. I was about to weep musky tears of lust, when she slipped it out again, leaving me begging inside.

Alex gave me a goofy smile.

"Your turn," she said then rolled onto her back and pulled me on top of her. I was confused by this sudden shift, but Alex repositioned our hips from below, and we were completely touching, skin to skin.

"Go ahead, now you can enjoy me," she said to my utter embarrassment. My jaw dropped when I heard that, but before I could wiggle away, just to give my mind a break, Alex started moving my hips. I had to grip onto the sheet as the sensual heat rushed up from my opened thighs. A moan escaped my lips. She finally got me stirring on my hot wetted sex against hers.

"Enjoy the ride," Alex teased. Our breasts brushed over each other. My hair flew down to Alex's bare chest. The burning pleasure poked at me from the inside, causing me to let loose a wash of slippery, scented juice. Alex inhaled deeply as if she was also taken by the overwhelming joy we were creating. Her hands kept squeezing around my churning back cheeks. Alex gasped, her mouth went ajar. I couldn't help feeling even more hyper to see her arousal as strong as mine.

I had never felt so wild and so free, like being on top of the world, even it was just being on top of Alexandra. Until an orgasm the size of an entire forest hit me, I almost tore the sheet out of the bed. Alex held me when I collapsed onto her. She rubbed my back as I panted.

"Want more?" Alex asked. I thought she was joking, but she just rolled me onto my back and I felt the weight of her body on me again. She kissed my chest and my stomach. Her fingertips glided up and down over my pink femininity and my heavily soaked opening. My feral heated walls were screaming to be filled with those long lithe fingers. Alex's mouth wrapped around my hot swollen pearl. Her frenzy slithering tongue rubbed over me until I whimpered. All the while, she moved her fingers inside my warm dripping folds, swirling about and whipping my scent into the air.

I choked on the endless pleasure as Alex continued teasing. I just wanted to beg for her to do me already. Then when I least expected it, she plunged two slender fingers inside my craving wetness. The inside of my hips shivered, feeling her entire finger length buried deep into me. I found her mouth nibbling on my heated pearl again. Alex started moving her hand, slowly and cautiously and then became more urgently. My whole body was shaking with pleasure.

When my muscle started trembling and I started screaming from sheer pleasure, Alex had to actually cover my mouth to quiet me, holding me down to stop me from squirming away at the intensity. My fingernails were digging into the bed as her teeth were on me. I wanted to beg her to stop and not to stop at the same time.

When the sensation became too powerful, the hot flaming joy erupted between my spread legs. It came rushing throughout my body like a wildfire. I had to keep myself from passing out from too much carnal bliss.

Alex kept her hand moving even as I came all over her. The feeling was beyond description. I didn't know who or where I was anymore.

Until she was sure it was over that she slipped her fingers out of me. I winced a little to that wonderful aftertaste. A smile lighted Alex's face as she looked down at her hand. I couldn't be more embarrassed, because when she held her palm up, turning it around, and I saw my clear slimy juice dripping down her elbow. I was surprised at how hard Alex had made me come this time.

"Mmm...You taste like sweet peaches," she said, licking her soaked fingers. I blushed and buried my face in a pillow. Alex giggled and dropped down beside me, pulling me into her arms.

CHAPTER 27

Time moved slowly yet passed quickly. While Alex was preparing for the trip to Moscow, I spent my time with other slaves in the house. Although I was no longer restricted as one of them, I was still a human, and I needed human companions.

But once I got into the kitchen, I was shell-shocked by the sight of my fellow servants. They looked like lifeless zombies, too pale, skinny and worn-out, I almost couldn't recognize them all. My heart sank. I was the only one in the house that didn't share the horrible look.

As I stepped toward them, they looked at me with those sunken eyes.

"What are you doing here, Avery?" a girl asked me in a weak voice. I remembered her name was Lisa. She was the one that told me about her brother who got sent away to the human farm.

"What happened to you, Lisa?" I said with concerns. "You don't look well."

She didn't say anything, but something in her eyes showed me her fear and misery.

"Is it the new mistress Nikol?" I asked again.

"Please, don't mention her name. We don't want to get into trouble," Lisa said nervously. "You shouldn't be here. We're serving our blood for the breakfast. She'll need me at the east wing soon."

Suddenly, I felt seriously sick and angry. But I knew I couldn't do anything about it, which was why it frustrated me even more. Lisa turned to a tray of wine glasses mixed with fresh blood. When she held her hands out, I caught a glimpse of her wrists. There were more scares than I could count. Her neck and shoulders also covered in bruises and pink scars that looked like animal bites. The girl looked so weak and so pale.

"Tell me, Lisa," I said. "How many times does she feed on you?"

"I'm sorry, Avery, I have to bring my blood in by now, I can't be late," she just said, but when she started to walk, her knees buckled. I rushed to her side, took the tray of blood from her and helped her to sit down.

"You're not well. You can't go like this."

"What else can I do? I don't want to be punished," she said helplessly.

"I...I'll take the blood there for you," I found myself speaking.

"Really? Are you sure?" Lisa looked at me in surprise, but I could tell she was also somewhat relieved from the burden. I knew I couldn't back down either.

"Yes." I nodded. "Leave it to me."

"No, no, you don't have to. You're not with us anymore."

I hated being treated as a slave, but now I realized I also hated not being anything in particular, neither slave nor free. I swallowed back the feeling and looked at the girl in the eyes.

"Lisa, it's alright. I'll go very quickly, and I would be careful, alright?" I said. The girl nodded, and I took the tray then left the kitchen.

I reached the east wing of the mansion where Nikol's room was and also Anastasia's. I knew they shared the chamber together and everything, but some stupid part of me wanted to take the risk.

"Well, to hell with it," I muttered to myself.

Then I pushed open the grand door of their room. The room was enormous, just like Alex's. But it looked more decorative with pieces of landscape paintings and artistic objects hanging around. I walked inside with a lump stuck in my throat. The voice inside my head told me to get out of there, but my heart kept pushing me in. Even I knew Nikol was there, I was still hoping to see Anastasia, at least just a little.

There was no sound inside. Curiosity got the best of me. I walked toward the bedroom. The door wasn't locked. I pushed it gently and then I saw them. They were both asleep in bed, but the worst part that I didn't expect to see they were both naked. Their hair cascaded over each other's body so perfectly; they looked like they were in a classic painting. The way Nikol placed her head on Ana's chest, a satisfied look on her sleeping face made my heart drop. How would I feel to see my lover passionately made love with someone else? I'd never felt so hurt and so livid. I just wanted to throw up.

Soon, burning tears rolled down my cheeks. Even I wanted so badly to leave; I couldn't make my legs move.

Then Anastasia's golden eyes flared open as if she'd sensed someone in the room. I jolted back in surprise, causing the wine glasses to clink together. The sound made her look in my direction. A shock registered on her face when she saw me. I put the tray on the table by the door and ran out of the room.

My body felt anesthetized and weighty as I was struggling to keep my legs moving. I had to concentrate so hard not to fall. Every step I took, I kept telling myself over and over that I was stupid, stupid, stupid! Why did I even come here?

I ran along the hallway and down the staircases. The sound of faraway footsteps came after me, and I heard her calling my name, but I ignored the silky voice. I just wanted to keep running like that until I reached the end of the world.

Two strong arms grabbed me by the waist, pulling my body to a halt. It felt as if I had run into an iron chain.

"Let me go!" I cried, twisting around and trying to push the hands away.

"Avery! Shhh! Please stop! Listen to me!" Ana's voice tried to calm me.

"It doesn't matter anymore!"

"Avery, it's not like what you think!" Anastasia said. She dragged me away from the hall before she let me go. I turned myself around to see that beautiful face again. She was in her flowing nightgown. I could feel her soft breasts against my body. Her hair didn't look like she'd just rolled out of bed to catch me in the hallway at all. The silky golden waves twirled around her shoulders, covering her stunning body.

But when I looked into those gorgeous golden eyes, I felt all the hurt doubled.

How it pained me to imagine someone else's hands had touched her beautiful form nights and days.

"Avery, you have to understand that it's not what I want."

"Oh right, so I'm supposed to say sorry. I'm sorry for waking you up after a sweet sleepless night with your lover. I'm sorry for being a nosy stupid human sla—"

I would've kept going forever if Anastasia didn't push me into a corner and kissed me hard, I couldn't talk. The kiss was so sudden and rough. Her soft lips moved over mine. The sweet smell of her breath caught in my mouth. For a moment, I could almost smell the scent of Nikol on her skin. Anger writhed through my veins again. I pushed Anastasia away and slapped her face. Ana's head turned to the side at the force. Her jaw hardened. I immediately regretted it.

Anastasia turned back to look at me. My hands already went to my mouth in shock.

"Oh my god...I'm so sorry, I didn't mean to. I'm sorry, Anastasia," I came to apologize.

"Avery, I wish I knew how to make you trust me. But I love you, not Nikol, and I'm not going to change a single word I've said, you have to believe me." She looked me straight in the eyes. I could see her golden pupil widened and glowed. "How could I lose the only person I've ever loved in my life?" she added in a softer tone.

"But it hurts so much," I said and burst into tears. Anastasia pulled me into her again. She held me against her chest and stroked my hair. I felt a kiss on the top of my head as we hugged.

"I'm so sorry, Avery. It hurts me too."

CHAPTER 28

The hot water washed over my skin. Warm droplets formed steam as I stood there without moving at all. The voices kept banging inside my head. They said the same thing, over and over again, how much clearer could it be? What was going on with my life?

My skin was burning from the mellow droplets morphing into sharp little blades of fire. I pulled myself back together again and left the shower. Drying my dark brown hair, wrapped myself in a white bathrobe before stepping out of the misty shower.

As soon as I got out, it was like a lightning bolt struck. Nikol was sitting on my bed with her long legs crossed. The only thought that ran through my mind was, "I'm going to die." Her cold violet eyes sent a chill down my spine. Suddenly, she rushed forward and pushed me back into the bathroom. She slammed the door shut behind us.

Nikol gripped me by the hair, dragging me across the floor. Then she threw me onto a small table by the bathtub. I tried to get up but she held me down and rolled me onto my back to face her. Her hand clasped over my mouth, preventing me from screaming. She bent over. Her dangerous face was very close to mine.

"Slave girl, you certainly are an impressive one. I must have forgotten to make my point clear, but you should've known better than that. Why is it hard to understand that I will kill anyone who lusts after Anastasia, let alone a slave like you?" Nikol said, staring into my eyes, making my heart skip a lot of beats. I squirmed in panic as Nikol observed me for a moment then tilted her head to the side in a questioning way.

"I wonder why not only Anastasia but also Alex. What's so special about you anyway?" she mused. "Oh is it the blood?"

My terror rose up at her words. Nikol flashed her perfect teeth at me. My eyes widened as I saw her white canines growing out an inch long. I wiggled away, trying to move Nikol off my body, but she kept holding me down with her strong hands. I tried to scream through my clasped mouth, but the only sounds I made were muffled whimpers.

My cries were useless.

"I think I would like to find out." Nikol pulled her crimson lips and yanked the collar of my robe open. Then she bit down into my exposed neck. The piercing pain burst through my skin like hot fire. I tried to scream from the burning agony.

It was like being bitten by a venomous snake. Tears welled up and rolled off the corner of my eyes. I could feel my blood being drained out of my veins so fast, a wave of dizziness enveloped me. I thought I was going to faint, but Nikol finally broke off. She grunted and licked her blood-stained lips.

"Oh my, did I hurt you?" she said through her sharp teeth. "Sorry you poor thing, I have to admit you taste so darn good. Well, curse my appetite, but shall we have another sip?"

The warm blood kept oozing down my throbbing wound. The metallic scent clogged my nostrils. This made Nikol's eyes stirred with uncontrollable thirst. I tried to beg with my teary eyes, but the look on her face was full of blood lust now. It was the vampire thing after all.

Nikol bared her teeth again and sank her dagger-sharp fangs into my already burning flesh. The pain was insane. My whole body writhed in madness under her. I gave up crying for help and started wishing for death instead. This was much to bear, and slowly, my brain started numbing some part of my body.

My vision began to darken as Nikol kept drinking me lustfully.

But out of nowhere, a flash of motion whizzed past us, and Nikol's weight was lifted off my body. My legs gave way, and I slipped from the table to the floor. Alex already pinned Nikol against the wall, lifting her off the floor by the throat.

"How dare you!" Alex growled in a hot fury. Her vampire fangs extended from her upper jaw in full length. Her heated golden eyes burned with a murderous look. Nikol struggled to free herself, but Alex was too strong. She made the concrete wall crack behind Nikol. It seemed like Alex was trying to push Nikol through the wall. But at the same time, I felt something warm running down the inside of my throat. I choked and then coughed up a mouthful of blood into my palm.

Alex instinctively turned back to me. A frightened look I'd never seen from her appeared on her face. She released Nikol and quickly came to my side.

"Avery!" Alex cried and pulled me into her arms, resting my head on her chest. "Avery, please no, please! Stay with me!"

But I felt so cold and my eyelids felt so heavy. I just couldn't stop myself from sinking into a deep darkness.

CHAPTER 29

I opened my eyes again. A blurry form hovered over me. When the haze cleared away, I realized I was on the bed with Alex sitting beside me.

"Hey... you're awake, sleepyhead," she said softly, leaning herself over to study my face. Her eyes were full of gentleness and concerns. She smoothed my hair and smiled. "How are you feeling, princess?"

I frowned, trying to notice my own feelings. I thought I was fine until a sharp pain stirred up from the crook of my neck again, and I remembered how I got it. I had just survived Nikol's bite, but the stinging feeling was still bothersome.

"I'm hurt," I croaked helplessly.

"I know, sweetheart, I know," Alex cooed and stroked my cheek with the back of her hand. "It was a nasty cut, but you'll be up and running in no time. I had given you my blood to heal your wound. "

"Yuck," I said and winced again. Alex giggled and kissed my forehead.

"You just need to take some rest," she said and then gave a heavy sigh again. "I wish I could stay here with you longer, but I have to go."

"What about Nikol?" I asked. A dark shadow crossed Alex's face.

"She's alive now because I'm not done with her yet," she said. "But don't worry. I won't let anyone hurt you again."

"It's my fault, Alex," I said. "Nikol didn't mean it."

"Did she hit your head too?" Alex said.

"No, I meant, she's just jealous, because—Anastasia and I—we—we're still seeing each other."

I was bracing myself for Alex's bursting tantrum, but it didn't come. Instead, Alex kept staring at me with those steady golden eyes. I expected her to get up and storm off the room, but she just sat there looking at me for a long time.

"Say something Alex, you're scaring me," I said in a pleading voice. Alex sighed again.

"I wish I knew how to make you want to be with me, Avery," she said. "I hope it makes everything crystal clear when I'm not pressuring you anymore. I love you too much. I could die seeing you get hurt."

"Oh Alex, I'm so sorry," I said. Tears threatened to roll down my cheeks. "I don't know what to do."

"You'll be fine. Anastasia will take care of you when I'm gone," she said to my surprise. I stared up at her, trying to figure out what had happened during my state of unconsciousness.

Alex moved over and got into bed beside me. She pulled me gently into her warm embrace. I rested my head on her chest and she caressed my back and smoothed my hair.

"Today, I've learned the most important truth," she whispered in my ear. "That I can really lose what I cling onto. So now I have to let you go. That way I will always remember you as my perfect love, the one I will cherish forever in my heart. I don't care what your decision is. Whether you choose to be with me or Anastasia, I will still love you, always."

I wasn't sure of what she was trying to get at, but I had a terrible feeling gnawing at me. I had no idea why it felt like I had done something wrong, except I didn't know what exactly I had done.

CHAPTER 30

ALEXANDRA

After Avery fell asleep again, I untangled myself from her arms and got out of bed carefully. She looked so peaceful when she slept. Her skin glowed under the beams of a morning sun. Those long thick lashes damped with crystalline tears just broke my heart. I stared at her adorable face, tracing my eyes to her soft inviting full lips. How those lips always tickled my inside when we kissed. I wanted so badly to place mine on hers again but dared not to for fear of waking her from this beautiful slumber.

At last, I was able to tear my eyes away from her face and left the room.

When I stepped outside the door, Anastasia was right in front of me.

"How is she?" she asked.

"Where's Nikol?"

"Let me in. I want to see Avery," she said and started to move, but I gripped her arm. I clenched my jaw to calm myself though I was trying my hardest not to throw my sister across the hall. Anastasia finally looked back at me.

"You know who brought this to her, don't you?" I said through my teeth.

"I did warn you about Nikol, didn't I?"

A fury burst through me. I flashed forward and shoved Ana against the far wall. My hands closed around her throat, but Anastasia didn't even flinch in fright. Instead, she looked at me calmly.

"How dare you say that to me?!" I hissed.

"Everything happened because of you, Alex," Anastasia spat back.

I just wanted to rip my sister apart, but deep down I knew she was right. She was right all along. Nikol's attack wasn't Anastasia's fault, it was mine. I was selfish to keep Nikol around, just so Anastasia couldn't get Avery back. I was scared of losing her as she said. We stared at each other, and after a long stretching moment, I took a deep breath and released my sister.

"Avery's asleep," I said in a low voice. "You can see her unless I'm out of here."

Then Victor came walking toward us. He bowed at me and cleared his throat.

"My lady, everything is all set," he said.

"Good, but I still have one more thing to deal with."

I turned to walk to the east wing. Anastasia's eyes lighted up. She knew what I was going to do with Nikol, and I had to give her the satisfaction of being right.

I walked into their mansion with my sister following behind me. Then I pushed opened the grand door.

Nikol was sitting on the sofa like an arrogant queen. She didn't bother to look up from her cup of jasmine tea when I approached her. Anastasia gripped my elbow.

"Sister, please don't." She shook her head at me. If it wasn't for the fact that Nikol shared a long line of history with us, I would have killed her twice today. I brushed Anastasia's hand aside and walked over to her. My eyes stared down at the top of her head. Nikol looked up at me and smirked.

"What are you going to do to me, Alexandra?" she asked, putting her teacup down on the table. "It's quite funny, don't you think? You got all worked up because of a human slave."

My hand grabbed Nikol by the throat then slammed her head against the couch. Her violet eyes widened in shock.

"You go back to Kremlin with me, Nikol!" I snarled.

"What?!" she said through her tight throat.

"You heard me."

"You can't do this to me, Alex!"

"I can and I will!" I snapped. "Now shut up and get out of this house before I rip your head off!

Nikol stared back at me with her furious violet eyes. Her sharp canines were drawn out in defense, but she knew she had to obey me.

I let her go at last. Nikol coughed with a sour expression and rolled her head around as if to see whether it still worked. I guessed I almost broke her neck somehow, and a part of me wished I had.

When I turned around to walk away, Nikol stood up.

"Are you going to let them be together like that, Alexandra?" Nikol snapped. Anastasia turned her face to look at me, but my eyes drifted back to Nikol again.

"I trust the one I love," I said and then left the room.

CHAPTER 31

AVERY

Anastasia sat on the bed beside me when I woke up the second time. She gave me a sweet warming smile as I stared back at her in surprise. Her blonde lock fell loose over her shoulders in all the right places. She looked like an angel. Those deep golden eyes sparkled as she studied me.

"Anastasia," I breathed.

"Hello, love," she whispered back.

I sat bolt upright from the bed. My hands reached for her elegant body. Ana moved over and let me hold her in my arms.

"Be careful, my love, you're still recovering," she said softly into my hair.

"Tell me it's not a dream," I said, tightened my embrace around her. I felt her hands stroking my back.

"No, it's not," she said and pulled away with a smile. "Here we are again, here and now, that's all there is."

Then she brought her soft tender lips to mine. I had missed this slow light kiss from her. I kissed Anastasia's sweet scented lips back. After a while, we broke off and gazed into each other's eyes. Our foreheads met in contentment. I touched her face, running my thumbs over her smooth cheeks. Her thick silky blonde lock brushed against my forearms as we sat facing each other. It felt so familiar and welcoming.

128

"Forgive me," Anastasia whispered, her exquisite breath caressed my lungs as she spoke. "I promise I will never leave you ever again."

"I love you," was all I could muster up to say.

"I love you more," she said and leaned in for my lips again. Then the thought of Alex hit me. It was like a jab of a needle in the back of my mind that I had to jolt back from Anastasia.

"What's wrong?" she frowned.

"Oh... I just remember...how about Alex and Nikol?"

"There's no one here now," Ana reassured me, putting her delicate finger under my chin, "Just the two of us."

She smiled again and continued to close the distance between us until our lips touched. But my mind was still wondering about Alex. Why did she leave without saying a goodbye? I knew she was going to, but it still felt strange that she just left like that. An unknown feeling seemed to poke around from the deep of my chest, and it made me feel uneasy inside. But I couldn't wrap my mind around it yet. Perhaps I needed sometimes to adjust to this new reality, that now I had Anastasia back in my arms again. I pushed the thoughts of Alex away. At last, I was able to be with the love of my life, and it was all that mattered.

"Can we move out of this room?" Ana said with a grimace. "I don't want to stay in Alex's place too long. I can get suffocated in here."

"Oh?" I said

"How about coming to my chamber instead?" she said and smiled brightly.

"Yes, wherever you want." I smiled back.

CHAPTER 32

ANASTASIA

Avery was still sleeping when I placed a tray of breakfast on the bed. I moved over to her and kissed her bare shoulder. She didn't stir. Her back was still turned to me. I got on top of her and kissed her cheek over and over until she frowned and rolled onto her back. Yet Avery still didn't show any sign of waking up. She was so adorable. I giggled to myself and brushed a strand of hair from her face. I'd never seen a person looked so lovely while sleeping. I could watch her like that all day. But then I would crave her company so much, I would have to be selfish and bring her back to the waking world with me.

I needed her. I needed her like the earth needed the sun.

I leaned to kiss her again on the lips.

"Rise and shine, beautiful," I whispered against her skin. Avery finally opened her eyes and blinked a few times before she looked at me. I smiled and kissed her cheek again.

"Anastasia?" she said sleepily.

"Good morning sunshine. Sorry to wake you up, but I just couldn't wait to hear your voice," I said. I was ready to claim her mouth when Avery covered her face with her hands.

"Aw...why?" I raised an eyebrow at her.

"I'm a human," she said, peeking through her fingers at me.

"So?" I frowned.

"I have morning breath.

I burst out laughing.

"And I'm a vampire, remember?" I said, "So you always smell delicious to me."

"Ew!" she grimaced. I laughed again and pulled her hands away and kissed her full on the lips. I loved kissing Avery. She had the best reaction in the world. I loved the tilt of her head, her soft inward breath, and her lovely blush. The feeling of her soft lips touching and becoming one with mine was all priceless.

After a while, we pulled away.

"I made you breakfast," I said and got off her again. Avery sat up as I tugged some pillows for her to lean on. I brought in the tray of fresh fruit and pancakes. I even made a smiley face from rich whip cream and blueberries on top. The strawberries were cut in halves to look like beautiful heart shapes around the plate. Avery giggled when she saw my design.

"You made this by yourself?" she asked.

"Sure did," I said. "Almost gave the cooks a heart attack when I entered the kitchen."

Avery giggled lively again. I poured some syrup over the pancakes for her and watched her took the first bite.

"How was it?" I asked eagerly.

"It tastes delightful, thank you." She smiled back. "But I can't eat if you keep watching me like that." She noticed me eyeing her with intense interests.

"Alright, how about this?" I moved over to sit behind her then wrapped my arms around her waist and rested my chin on her shoulder. "Now you don't see me and you can eat in peace."

Avery laughed a musical laugh. She shook her head and turned around to peck me on the cheek. I kissed her neck back and let her continue eating. I just wanted to be like this with her every single day. I would make her breakfast every morning and we could just stay in bed cuddling each other all day.

My eyes checked on the pink scars on Avery's neck. The bite marks from Nikol's attack was still visible. It hurt me so much just to imagine the pain she'd gone through. I claimed it was Alex's fault, but I knew it was mine too. We both hurt Avery one way or the other. I would never let anyone hurt her again. I kissed her scars lightly, wishing the pain to go away.

Avery turned to me again with bright childish eyes. She held a strawberry to my lips, but I just looked at it and shook my head back.

"Please, this one tastes lovely," she urged with a smile. I rolled my eyes at her. Sometimes, Avery seemed to forget what I was, but I opened my mouth and bit onto the red juicy fruit anyway. But the movement of my upper jaw squeezed the fangs to slide out of my gum, but I drew them back quickly. Yet Avery had already noticed them. She put her fork down and lowered her gaze.

"Did I scare you?" I asked.

"No, no, Anastasia, I was just wondering," she said and turned to look into my eyes. "When Nikol bit me, it hurt so much; I thought I was going to die. But why having vampire blood in my system could heal me so fast?"

I frowned at her sudden interest in it, but I understood her human curiosity.

"Blood is the essence to all livings," I said. "Our race drinks human blood to survive, but we also produce our own from the amount of blood we feed on. My metabolism is different from yours. You get energy from food and turn it into blood cells. We get it directly from your blood cells. In other words, our systems create a unique essence from a unique species. That's why vampire blood can be so revitalizing."

"No wonder why Alex's worked like a charm," she pointed out. "I can't feel the pain anymore. I feel normal now."

"Yes, you're right," I said. "Alex and I are a bit different from the rest."

"Oh in regard that you're a royal and you turned by yourself," she said knowingly. I tilted my head to the side.

"How did you know so much about that?"

"Alex told me," she said with a shrug.

"So, you guys talked a lot, huh?" I said. Avery stared at me, now that I sounded a bit jealous, but she dropped her face and looked away.

"Alex wants to turn me, you know that?" she said. "But why did you object her?"

"You don't know how we create vampires, do you?" I asked. Avery shook her head. I sighed again and brushed my thumb over the corner of her lips.

"We have to keep drinking from the person until that person is fully transmitted with enough venom that it will start to change the system slowly," I explained. "And at the last stage of turning, the vampires have to let the victim drink their blood, but this process has to be done instantly and without any interruption or the human will die. Not everyone is successfully turned, Avery."

"So that means it's a fifty-fifty chance?" she said. "Anyway, don't laugh, but can vampires be killed by drawing a wooden stake into their hearts?"

I couldn't help burst out laughing at that.

"That's rude!" Avery scolded me with a glare. "When someone asks you not to laugh, you're not supposed to!"

"Well sorry, but I just think that anything would die if you drew a stake— wooden or not, through its heart. Sure, you can kill a vampire in this way, but you can also kill anyone in that way, too."

"I thought you were immortal," she said.

"Yes, we are. We can live until the end of time, but that doesn't mean we're not killable," I said truthfully.

For a moment, Avery's face seemed quite sad. I knew she was being sensitive, but I found it a little strange.

"Are you alright, sweetheart?" I asked, looking at her with concerns.

"Yes, I'm fine," she said and tried to smile again, but the smile didn't seem to reach her eyes. "I think I need a shower now."

"Oh, alright then." I nodded and released her from my arms. I watched Avery moving away until she disappeared into the bathroom. Maybe I worried too much. She was fine now. We were together again at last.

CHAPTER 33

AVERY

I stepped out of the bathroom again after a long shower. Then I saw Anastasia walking into the room, holding some clean clothes in her hands. When her face turned to me, she froze and then dropped the clothes to the floor. I was wrapped in a towel and still dripping with water. The light in Ana's golden eyes shifted. It was my turn to freeze in place, wondering what I did wrong.

"Er...I don't have any clothes with me, so..." I tried to explain, thinking it was inappropriate to walk around half-naked. But before I could blink, Anastasia was already in my face.

My stomach did a flip. I recognized that look, that hungry look that had nothing to do with my blood. Anastasia pushed me to the wall and wrapped her mouth around my lips. She kissed me greedily like she had been starving for so long. I was half-startled and half-satisfied by her sweet assault. I sensed the heat of lust started to rise from our craving bodies.

Anastasia pinned me flat against the wall. She lifted one of my legs up and hung it over her raised knee, and just like that, I was completely spreading for her. In a standing position, I could feel the heat coursing inside me. Her hands roamed under my towel, feeling around my damped body.

She tugged my towel away, leaving my naked body unprotected and even more aroused.

Ana's fingers explored their ways over my swelling pink flesh. I realized I already anticipated her invasion. She found my slippery drooling passage and slid her fingers through it. I gasped out loud and lost my breath again. My heart bit fast and hard. My hips bucked instinctively to the unexpected invasion. The pleasure wracked through my body. Anastasia kept delving deeper, trying to find my weakest spot. I dropped my jaw in a blissful joy.

"Oh my god, Anastasia...!" I cried her name, trying to cling on to her. My fingernails clawed her shoulders, but there was no turning back for both of us.

"I'm sorry, Avery, I just can't wait to have you again. I've missed you so much. I just can't," she whispered against my skin. Our bodies entwined. My mind couldn't focus on anything except the sensitive region between my spread legs. The inside of my walls shivered with a burning desire. I thought I was going to come with just the insertion alone. She distracted me by running her lips over mine. She got us into another tongue-braiding kiss.

She moved down to lick my red hardened nipples and caressed my aching breasts with her free hand. My eyes rolled back as my body became hypersensitive. I felt her inside me, awakening my tingling wet cavern. I knew it was time. The wonderful movement started. My purring hot sex got hotter each time Ana gave her tender slow thrust. It was as if she was probing for something hidden inside, trying to reach up to unlock the orgasmic treasure chest in the depth of my walls.

My slipperiness soaked everything in contact. I moaned shamelessly to the endless sensual bliss. My legs started to shake against Anastasia's. She was driving me crazy with her non-stop deep-drilling. With an indescribable pleasure, she ripped open the ecstatic universe between my opened thighs. I screamed like a wild animal from the powerful eruption. My body rippled and wriggled against Anastasia's. I felt my dripping flesh constricted around her fingers as I came.

Anastasia wrapped one arm around my waist and pulled me back to her. I rested my head on her shoulder and panted heavily, trying to catch my breath.

After the mind-blowing eruption subsided, she whispered in a polite tone, "May I?"

I gave a weak nod but had to brace myself when she slipped out of me again.

"I love you, Avery, remember that," Anastasia said and kissed my neck. I never knew there was this unpredictable side of her. I wasn't sure I could ever get used to it.

CHAPTER 34

NIKOL

I found myself inside a black after our private jet landed. We were heading towards the Red Square. Being forced to come back to this frozen city with Alex made everything seem irritating to my eyes. Rubber tires made crunching sounds over the ice as a parade of royal cars crawled into the quiet capital. People used to roam around this place, but not anymore. Moscow was now like a ghost city after the war, but I liked it that way. The limo kept rolling on a snow-packed street until the great Kremlin Wall came into view.

I glanced at Alexandra, who was sitting like a stone status by the foggy window. She had been ignoring me for this whole boring trip. How could she do that while I couldn't bear the thought of leaving Anastasia to that human girl? Alex was so stupid to leave them together. I should have killed the girl when I got the chance. Now I had to find a way to get back to Anastasia. Then I would prove to her that I was worthy of her than that slave. I would make her mine again.

The only person standing in my way right now was Alex. She wasn't going to make it easy for me. Yet I had my plans. If all else failed, there would still be a backup plan for me.

I wouldn't let them treat me like I was nothing.

Turning around to Alex, I decided to move closer to her. She didn't notice me, so I lifted one of my legs onto the seat and stretched the other over her lap. Alex jumped up. She snapped her head to me, arching her perfect eyebrows in a question.

"What are you doing?"

"Getting your attention?" I said with my most seductive tone. Alex rolled her eyes and shook her head. I wouldn't let her ignore me like that.

"I can't believe you're doing this to me, Alex," I said, bringing my face closer to her cheek. My lips brushed over her skin. I twirled her collar shirt with my fingers. "Don't you know it's killing me to be away from my lover? And I can't guarantee that I would stay sober around you."

"No wonder why my sister is scared of you, Nikol," Alex said without looking at me. I clenched my jaw, trying not to let it affect my mood. I moved over Alex and straddled on her lap. My feminine part poked at her stomach through the soft fabric of my underwear. I already felt the wetness stirred up inside me as I looked at those captivating golden pools. I almost forgot how stunning this arrogant princess was. Alex's expression was a mixture of surprise and annoyance, but I wouldn't give her a chance to push me off. My lustful lips nipped on her neck as my body started to grind against her lower part.

"Nikol! What the—!" Alex said, frantically leaning herself back when my tongue invaded her mouth. I snaked my hand inside her pants, but before I could reach her private, Alex grabbed my wrist and turned me over. My back landed on the seat. I tried to get up, but Alex held my shoulders down. Her face hovered over mine.

I licked my lips, trying to hide a smirk. I knew even the great Alexandra Romanov couldn't resist me. My possessive arms wrapped around her swan-like neck. My tight skirt was rolled up, showing off my black lingerie and sexy long legs. I didn't even hesitate to wrap them around her waist, too. As our bodies touched, I could feel my own nipples erected under my silk bra. The heat exuded from my lustful flesh between my thighs. One touch from Alex's delicate hand would send me off to the sky.

"Why don't we work together Alex? You can have the girl when I get Anastasia back. Wouldn't you like that?" I asked in a whisper, breathing my seduction into every word.

"Thanks for your glorious idea, Nikol, but your charms don't seem to work on me," Alex said to my surprise and got off again, leaving me speechless and humiliated.

CHAPTER 35

We got out of the car at last. In front of the Royal Palace, black-coated soldiers stood at attention on both sides of the red carpeted pathway. I looked up at the multi-domed roof of the red majestic buildings before me.

A group of royal guards appeared and bowed at Alexandra. We kept walking forward through the massive gate. Then I saw a bearded man came up and gave a respective bow to Alex.

I recognized him. He was the *Starets*, a holy man, who had served as a religious teacher to the imperial family back in the day. I was a little surprised that this starets was still around. The former Czar was so fond of him. They thought his prayers had saved their sick Czarevich Alexei, who was the only heir to the Russian throne at that time. But the Bolsheviks thought they were just a bunch of lunatics. I guessed that was another reason why the Russian sovereignty took a nose dive.

But something else told me that I might one day need this person.

"*Velikaya Knyazna Alexandra*, Grand Duchess Alexandra, my apologies for this urgent meeting," the man said, addressing Alex by her royal title. I almost forgot Alex was, in fact, an imperial princess, higher in rank than other royal princesses in Europe. I used to feel gravely jealous of the Grand Duchesses as a young girl, but not anymore. Because why would I want to be like the duchesses when I could actually be on top of one? Or maybe I would be on top of them both.

The thought made me smile to myself. It was just a matter of time. When I could break Alexandra's shield, I would make her and her sister worship me for eternity.

"No need to be so formal, Rasputin," Alex said to the man, waving her hand off impatiently and continued to walk onward. "I need to know everything before sunset. You'd better make my stay worthwhile."

"Indeed, your highness." Rasputin bowed again. Then his crafty violet eyes caught mine, I gave him a flirtatious smile. He frowned at me a little before turning back to walk with Alexandra.

As we strode through the Portrait Hall of the Palace, Alex abruptly stopped and stared at a huge golden-framed painting of a woman on the wall. I followed her gaze. The painting was of Empress Alexandra Feodorovna in a massive imperial tiara made of diamonds and pearls.

If I wasn't mistaken, the priceless tiara was probably from the era of Catherine the Great. The woman was adorned in a heavily embroidered court gown and the scarlet ribbon. I secretly wondered where all those valuable treasures were kept right now.

Alex had her best face of stone as usual, but I knew what a mommy's girl she was.

"Czarina should have been here with us. She would be happy to see all this again," I said, gesturing to the whole place. "We got everything back. We have conquered the world and created a new one, didn't we, Alex?"

Alex's eyebrows furrowed for a minute and then turned to me sharply.

"No one should have been alive to see the hell we've created, Nikol," Alex said. "Why don't you go and entertain yourself? I've got work to do."

I wanted to say something nasty back, but I refrained myself. And all I could do was giving her a low hiss before clicking my heels off and out of the hall.

One day, I would make her sorry for keeping me imprisoned in this ghost palace of hers and for treating me like I wasn't half as good as her human slave.

I will make you pay, Alexandra, I thought to myself.

Some guards and royal maidens followed behind me. They ushered me to a guest chamber. When I got inside, my stomach growled out of sheer anger. My jaw throbbed. Damn, Alex had left me hot and bothered all by myself, and now I had to do something to release this stress.

"Bring me some humans," I said to the guards. "I want the healthiest ones you've got and make it quick."

The guards bowed before turning away.

I walked around the enormous room, tracing my eyes over the fine Italian interior decoration. The balcony view overlooked the Moskva River. I took off my long fur coat and settled on an armchair. A moment later, the guards reappeared. Two humans walked behind them, a boy in white shirt and knee-length pants and a girl in her neat maiden robe. My stomach rumbled at the sight of their healthy forms.

The guards gestured for them to get inside. Then they closed the heavy oak door and left. The girl and the boy tensed up when I rose from the chair. I looked at the girl. She had porcelain skin with yellow freckles and auburn hair. Such a cute face I'd got here.

"What's your name?" I asked her.

"Roza," she said. I admired her for being composed enough to answer me.

"Alright, I will get back to you later,"

Then I walked up to the boy. His baby face crumbled in fear. I clicked my tongue in sympathy as I stood in front of him.

"Oh sweetie, you are too young to die," I said, reaching my hand up to smooth the boy's blond hair. He flinched, but his blue eyes shone with a slight hint of hope. I smiled at him, loving how innocent he was.

"Where are you from, young man?" I asked.

"Fff...Frankfurt..." he stuttered.

"Ah nice! A German boy," I said and leaned over his shoulder to whisper in his ear. "Definitely my favorite taste."

The boy jolted back. His blue eyes went wide as he looked into mine.

"Don't be scared," I said. "How about this? We'll play a game. If you can reach the door before I could count to three, I'll let you live."

He swallowed hard. I knew this was cruel, but then who had power and didn't want to use it? I turned around, covering my face like I was playing peekaboo.

"Ready now? I'm counting. One—" I started. The sound of frantic footsteps echoed the room as the poor boy sprinted toward the door. My throbbing jaw squeezed the razor-sharp fangs out. I smiled to myself before uttering, "...three."

With my inhuman speed, I was able to block his path. The boy almost rammed into me.

"Oops, not so fast," I said, grabbing the back of his head and sinking my teeth into his exposed throat. I broke his vessels and started sucking his blood. The kid didn't even get a chance to scream let alone struggle against me. The girl gasped in horror as she witnessed this nightmarish scene. She fell to the floor with hysteric cries. My thirst was unquenchable. After a long moment, I dropped my young victim down. His body fell like a piece of rag to the floor completely drained of blood.

"Now it's your turn, baby," I said, licking my blood-smeared lips at the wild-eyed girl on the floor. She started to sob and beg. I walked up to her and grabbed her by the hair. She yelped, trying to pry my hand off. This reminded me of my time with Anastasia's love interest. How I wish the one in my hand right now was Avery. My adrenaline rushed, thinking of how I would torture her in my mind. Now Roza's screaming and begging only made me more excited. I dragged the girl toward the bed and threw her on it. She rolled onto her stomach and crawled to escape, but I got on top of her and grabbed her hair, pulling her head back.

"Not bad," I said, studying her porcelain face. "You look pretty. It would be a waste to kill you so soon. How about another game? If you can keep me entertained, I'll let you live. If not..."

I gripped her jaw and turned her head to the lifeless body by the door. "You know how it ends."

The girl seemed to take it all in. She stopped struggling and nodded, signaling her submission.

"Good girl," I said and ripped off her robe, tearing the fabric down her back until she was naked. I could see how she was becoming increasingly nervous. Her mortal heart pounded in my ears. My predatory side craved this kind of entertainment. I flipped her around to face me. My hands reached for her pale breasts, folding them until her nipples turned rosy red. Slowly her whimpers sounded with occasional moans. I snickered in amusement. Now I had found my personal sex slave. At least she could keep my mind off Anastasia and Alex for a while.

I traced my hand between her breasts, going over her smooth stomach and down to the sensitive femininity between her legs. My fingers parted her sweet tender lips. She gasped as I started poking lightly into her sex, provoking her sensual urges with gentle rubs over her rosebud. A rising lust replaced her fear, making her eyes glazed in joy. The girl had zero resistance. I wanted to know how long she would last. I shoved my middle finger through her warm virginity, a little too fast she yelped. But she clenched her teeth to muffle her cries. She probably remembered how she should behave. What a smart human girl. I kept going deeper. Her eyes fluttered open and close as her body felt my finger sliding in. I could sense that unmistakable sensation building up inside her hips.

I pulled my hand back and pushed two fingers into her again, her soft femininity swallowed them all the way in. I started wiggling inside her slippery walls, trying to find the most sensitive region within her honey hive. The girl bit her bottom lip and moaned. She was so tight and so sensitive down there, already shaking from a pleasurable lust. This made me realize she was still a virgin after all. What a toy I had found.

Pulling my fingers back, inch by inch until they were all the way out, I eased them back in deep into her wet virginity. My hand already got glistened from her arousal.

After a while, I increased the pressure and speed. She started trembling, enjoying a rippling and tingling feeling going through her body. The girl grabbed the bed sheet, crying and yet willingly spreading her legs wider for more. Every thrust seemed to engulf her in a flame of pleasure. I was right not to kill her off.

"Mm . . . mmm . . ." Roza's moans were becoming louder with every second, her freckled face flushed. Her back was slowly arching while her femininity became purring hot. The juices were trickling down between her thighs and dripping onto the bed. I was satisfied to see how wet I had made this innocent girl become. It was a real turn on to see her soaking entrance swallowing my fingers. I could already smell her arousal in the air around us.

After a few more frantic seconds, her breath caught in her throat and her body stiffened. I could feel her entrance tightened and constricted. It seemed like an electric shock went through her body. Her hips began bucking and her thigh muscles tensed up as she shook in obvious ecstasy. Small flicks of her juices were spitting out with every tug of my hand while I continued to push her over the edge.

"O...oh...god . . ." Roza was moaning from the intense pleasure as she had her first powerful orgasm ever in her life. Her back arched from the bed, twisting her body like a dying snake. I held her down and kept thrusting my hand into her until she rolled her eyes back. I enjoyed this sexual torture so much; I couldn't help laughing along the way. This was so much fun. I should do it often.

It was only until I stopped moving my hand that the girl's eruption subsided. Soon, her body relaxed and I pulled my cum-soaked fingers out of her, a little too fast, she yelped again. I snickered and put the glistened fingers into her mouth, telling her to lick them clean. Then I rolled back onto the soft bed and spread my own legs.

"Now show me how you can please me back, young lady," I said, smiling. Roza got up obediently and moved over to me. She was still nervous, but she had no right to protest. Slowly, she rolled up my leather skirt and pulled off my panties. She proceeded to give her best shot over my waiting hot sex. Her sleek tongue made its first lap over my already dripping lips. A low moan rose from my throat. Not bad for a then virgin, the girl had already passed her survival test.

CHAPTER 36

AVERY

In the semi-darkness of the room, our moaning sounded through the quiet night. The weight of an angelic figure atop me left no air in my lungs. I gasped as Anastasia ground herself against my heated pearl. She was taking her time, and it caused more slipperiness from my soaked entrance.

We both moaned in sensual pleasure. After a while, Ana lifted my knees up, spreading me wider. She went on to glide her fingers up and down, devouring my wet snub. She ran her other hand around my bum and sucked lightly on my neck, sending shivers up and down my spine.

My body trembled as she continued to lick my breasts, nibbling my throbbing nipples. Her fingers parted my moist lips and then slipped into my dripping slit without an effort. Like a key that always matched the lock.

The feeling of her sliding through my heavily soaked walls was priceless. My hands wrapped around Anastasia. My teeth clenched as I was breathing hard against her shoulder. Anastasia moved her hand, gently rocking me against the bed. My breasts flopped back and forth to the motion. I felt her tongue tracing my neck, causing goose bumps over my trembling body.

The heat started building up between my spread thighs. Then it was a little too much to handle. I couldn't pull myself back from reaching the edge.

My breathing came in raspy moans. My eyes kept rolling back as I sensed the pleasurable climax approaching.

"Oh...Ana.......Anastasia....I'm..." I cried. Then the muscles around my thighs tensed up as a delicious sensation exploded from the depth of my core. My legs stiffened out as I convulsed, throwing my head back. I let a scream as the wave of climax gripped my body, letting it sail over the edge of orgasm. Anastasia finally slowed down as I shuddered all over. My toes curled, unable to handle it anymore.

Ana withdrew her hand back from between my legs and came over to check on me. I couldn't wipe the daze of my eyes as I looked at her beautiful face again. She brushed a strand of hair from my face and tried to get me back to earth again with soft kisses on my neck. She looked down at me. The heat in her eyes making her irises glowed in the dark. For a brief second, it felt like a déjà vu. It kept creeping back into my mind like a boomerang. I turned to my side to avoid those fascinating golden eyes. They seemed to remind me of someone.

"Are you alright, baby? Did I hurt you?" Ana asked me in a voice of concerns. I shook my head, still clamped my hands between my legs over my throbbing girl flesh as I curled into a ball. It didn't hurt, but it felt too sensitive. My private place was still twitching from the effect of blissful sensation, I didn't dare to move.

"I'm fine. I just need a moment," I said, trying to recover. The area around my hips on the bed was wet from my juices. It showed just how much Ana made me respond to the all-consuming bliss.

Anastasia and I had been making love a lot since we were back together. It was like Anastasia never got tired of our sex. Sometimes, we were at it all day as if she was making up for the lost time. I was always on the verge of passing out each time she made me climax. Now I didn't think I would be able to handle it if she asked me to do it again. She gave more than I needed.

"It's alright, love. I won't touch you again, I promise," she reassured me, smiling. Then she leaned in to kiss my brow before rolling onto her back. Her hand reached out to stroke my cheek. Her steady golden eyes lingered on my face.

"I wonder who you take after. You look so beautiful, you know that?" she whispered. I couldn't help smiling in the dark.

"Not as beautiful as you are," I said, but Ana snorted.

"Did you know I was the ugliest among my siblings?"

"I don't believe it," I said.

"My sisters were all beautiful," Ana said. "They liked to tease us a lot when we were young."

"Us?"

"Me and Alex," Anastasia said. "We were called the Little Pair back then. We used to play together and shared each other's room. My older sisters, Titaina and Ogla were the Big Pair. They didn't like me, but they didn't mind Alex much."

I didn't know why the mention of Alex made my heart pound against my ribs.

"Why the difference?" I couldn't help being a little curious again.

"You wouldn't believe me," Ana chuckled. "Everyone thought I was a devil in the house."

"What? You being the little devil?" I said. "I couldn't picture that."

"Yes, it's the truth," Ana said with a small giggle. "I remember rolling a rock into my snowball and threw it at my older sister during a winter break in Poland. My father was so furious."

"You were indeed the nasty one," I chuckled.

"Yes I was," she agreed, laughing along. "But Alex wasn't like that. She was a good girl, always seeking to please, yet was constantly worried about not being loved enough."

I would never have guessed if Ana hadn't told me this about Alex. The cold-hearted person like Alexandra once cared too much. I already imagined the young Alex being sweet and caring. I had experienced her softer side sometimes, but I never thought it was really her true self.

"Please, stop talking about Alex," I said, "I just don't want to think about her."

Ana let out a low sigh.

"Avery, I know I had hurt you, but Alex was there to heal your broken heart. I'm not going to pretend there was nothing going on between you and my sister," she said. "I don't want to sugar-coat anything. When you know us clearly, you can decide who is best for you to be with."

"Oh Anastasia please, don't make me choose!" I blurted.

At that moment, Anastasia's eyes flickered to a different shade of emotion. It was like I had confirmed something she had dreaded for a long time. I was in shock myself. If I claimed to love only Anastasia, then why was I scared of having to choose? And when it all seemed too much, a burst of frustrating tears burned in my eyes. I buried my face in my hands and turned my back to her.

I hated myself for being like this. I hated hurting Anastasia, but I couldn't stop myself. Months ago if I was asked who I wanted to be with, the answer would be Anastasia without a doubt. But now I didn't have the clear answer anymore. After a while, I felt Ana's hands pulling me to her again. She tried to whisper something in my ear to soothe my raging sob. My shoulders shook as I cried. I knew I loved Anastasia so dearly, but then there was Alex.

Alex was always in my mind the whole time.

CHAPTER 37

NIKOL

I marched down the corridor between the rows of statues and tall windows, giving a half-hearted glance at the palace maids. They bowed when they saw me. Their red eyes beamed out in respect. The irony was I remembered growing up in an underprivileged home. Now everybody bowed at my feet.

The thought made me smile.

There were still a lot for me to be had. Blame it on my immortality. It had given me a freedom to get whatever I wanted, whenever I wanted. But nothing could compare to my longing for the Romanov sisters. They had it all. Any one of them in my grip would grant me everything I'd ever wished for. I would just have to work harder.

For many days I had wandered around Alex's palace all by myself. Most of the rooms were locked or abandoned, except the main ones. I had been looking for Alex all over the place, the imperial bedroom, the maple room, mauve room, the duchess's bedroom, and even Aleksey's playground. She wasn't in any of them. Then I decided to go over to where Czar Nicolas II's study was. There were so many guards standing at attention.

"Excuse me, ma'am, but you can't go in there," a soldier spoke to me. I looked back at him.

"Are you sure I can't go in, young man?" I said. The guards looked at each other nervously. They thought better of it and then stepped out of my way. These undead men need to learn some manners, I thought to myself.

Before I reached the massive door of Nicolas's room, I heard a conversation between Alex and another man.

"The hunters have killed our guards at the city border last night," the man, who I assumed was Rasputin, spoke. "I believe they are still lurking around the East gate."

"How many hunters do you think they have now?"

"Approximately a hundred or so," Rasputin said.

"A hundred? How could you let this going?"

"They're gathering more people to join their movement."

"Keep it as a secret," Alex said. "The humans should never know about this. What we don't want them to have now is hope. Don't let the hunters provoke them."

"Yes, your highness, but we can't keep it quiet for long," the man said again. "We need to annihilate the hunters to the root. They are a serious threat to us in the future."

"I know that," Alex exhaled. "But we need to have a well-planned strategy."

"What are we going to do then?"

"Let me think for a while," she said. "Now you may dismiss."

"Yes, Grand Duchess."

I heard footsteps and then the grand door groaned open and closed again. I walked toward the starets man. Then he turned and saw me, he frowned.

"I forgot to introduce myself," I said. "I'm Nikol Koreneva."

"I know you," the man said. "Your father worked for the Bolshevik."

He said the word like it was disgusting. I smiled seductively back, leaning myself forward him.

"And his daughter also works for the strong," I said, "You've got to be smart like us." I gave him a playful wink before pushing myself past the man and walked to the grand door. I could feel Rasputin's eyes stared at me.

Once I got inside the room and closed the door, I found Alexandra, sitting at her father's massive desk. A permanent scowl marred her face. When she saw me, she murmured something under breath. I couldn't help smiling, knowing that somehow, the two of us still shared a connection. The idea of being bound to Alexandra Romanov already caused a tingling sensation between my thighs.

I didn't bother with the pleasantries of "How are you". I just walked over to her antique desk and sat on it, crossing my long legs as I stared at her. Alex looked back at me with an annoyed look.

"Who let you in?" she said, looking at me as if I was some strayed animal.

"I let myself, why?"

"Go away, Nikol, I don't have time for your nonsense," she said in a flat tone.

"You can't just leave me alone all day, Alex," I pretended to whine. "I'm so bored in here."

She shook her head and continued to read over some maps on the table. I realized it was the map of Moscow.

"What are you doing? Planning another massacre?" I asked, trying not to sound too obvious that I'd been eavesdropping on her conversation with Rasputin earlier. Alex ignored me. I leaned myself over her shoulder, making sure my breast touched her faintly.

"You know, whatever you plan to do to the hunters, it won't work," I said. Finally, Alex turned to look at me again with interest.

"What are you talking about?"

I smiled as I knew I had gotten her full attention.

"They say to catch a tiger, you have to get to the jungle," I said. "But given the situation, you are the tiger now. The hunters are the ones to catch you."

"So you think you have a better idea?" she arched an eyebrow.

"A tiger can fake dead, you know," I said. "When they think they've got you, you can pull your hidden claws when they less expect it."

"I'm impressed, Nikol," Alex said. "How do you know so much about war strategies?"

"I'm not a general's daughter for nothing," I said, giving her a lustful wink. "Now for my useful input, can I get a reward for that?"

"Nikol," Alex said in a warning tone.

But I pulled her roller chair back and got on top of her in a straddling position. Alex wiggled her body away in surprise, but I wrapped my arms around her neck and clung to her tightly, bringing my face close to hers.

"Alex, if you let me go back with you, I promise to be a good girl," I whispered in her ear and nibbled her neck. "You can even have me anytime you want here, and I'll be happy to fill the role." I traced my lips along her perfect jawline. Alex turned her face away. She squeezed her eyes shut and sighed.

"For the last time, Nikol, you don't want to do this with me," she said, but I didn't stop what I had started. My hand reached down to slip my panties off from inside my tight skirt. I could feel the fabric parted my skin, leaving a wet feeling between my legs.

Alex opened her eyes again and looked up at me. Her face was unreadable. I tried to look into her golden irises, but there was no emotion of any sort. She was trying to act tough again. I spread my thighs and took her hand in mine.

"Take me any way you want, Alex," I whispered and guided her hand to my moist femininity. Once the tips of her delicate fingers touched my drooling pink flaps, all senses went abuzz. I inhaled, unable to believe myself that Alex actually let me go further at last.

My purring sex was already twitching and dripping as I slid Alex's hand over my sweet craving crack. I arched my breasts up to her face. They were already sprawling out through my unbuttoned shirt. My nipples hardened just at the touch of her breath on my skin.

I never knew having the Grand Duchess of Russia in my hand was more exciting than I expected. My body shivered in triumph. The feeling of her inside me almost made my mind swoon. I could feel my entrance getting wetter for her, luring her fingers to slip into me.

I guided her hand farther just enough to part my throbbing folds and let go. Alex suddenly gripped my waist and pulled me down, making my hips sink onto her. Almost by force, she pushed the whole length of her slender fingers through my warm wetness.

I gasped in shock. Confusion was written all over my face. A tingling feeling rushed through my hips as I felt her fingers sliding in. It made my thigh muscles jerk and shudder. My bottom clenched at her sudden penetration.

"Oh geez...Alex!" I whimpered and gasped harder. I could feel her all the way, going as far as she could. Her fingers swirled sensual inside my soaking walls. My juices trickled down my parted legs. It was overwhelming as my sensitive spot was being tickled and teased mercilessly.

The sensation inside my core started to weaken me, making me powerless in Alex's grip. She seemed to know exactly where to trigger it. I could feel her right at my orgasmic gate, and I was sure with a few little rubs, I would explode in ecstasy. But it looked like Alex had another plan, and I had a feeling that I wasn't going to like it.

"I told you, Nikol, you don't want to do this with me," she said and swiftly rose from her chair, lifting me off onto the table. Her body got between my spread legs as her hand was still secured deep inside my sopping walls. Alex brought her face closer to mine, grinning wide. Looking into her golden pools again, I gulped in panic. My heart pounded.

"What are you doing?" I was out of my breath. Everything looked hazy in my eyes. Every cell in my body went prickling.

"Isn't that what you wanted, huh?" she said and shoved her fingers deeper. The intense sexual feeling coursed through my body. The first thrust already poked my sensitive spot. I felt a jolt of electric sparks buzzed in my body. I hissed and moaned at the same time while Alex continued to tease. She pressed inside my softness, forcing me to the edge, but also not giving me enough to get over it. My body was burning hot. I was losing myself, losing control over the situation.

I could barely speak when her thumb rubbed against my burning pearl. And each time she hit the blissful region, I was engulfed in frenzy flames.

But Alex didn't seem to want to push me down the cliff of orgasm. She kept me stuck there, hanging over the edge. It was her way of torturing me. The more she moved inside my sensitive walls, the stronger my wanton needs became. It was too unbearable to the point that joyful tears started to well up in my eyes.

"You know what feels worse?" Alex said. "I could just pull out right before you could come and let you die inside, how

158

would you like that?" She said as she was inching out of me again. My eyes widened, realizing the terror.

"Oh, no! Alex, please, no! Don't do that," I begged, panting with desperation, feeling my arousal bubbling up from my sex pot. My juices flowed like there was no freaking dam.

"What did you say? I can't hear you over the sound of your moans," Alex teased, smiling wickedly down at me.

"I'm sorry, Alex," I apologized, finally surrendered. "I promise I will never do that again. Just let me have it now, please."

"Very well then," she said. "I assume you've learned your lesson."

Smiling, Alex eased her fingers back into me, increasing her speed. She started moving her hand furiously inside my walls. Wave after wave of bursting ecstasy rocked every part of my body, yet it felt like she was forcing me to come. I realized I was being forced to enjoy it against my will, and it was the most humiliating moment in my life. But I couldn't do anything about it.

My body shivered. I was heavily soaked from within. The tips of Alex's fingers tickled and nudged at my sensitive spot so repeatedly, a stirring climax threatened to break loose. And not before long, I could feel the powerful sensation coming like a tidal wave.

"Oh....Alex. . . Alex!!!"

The room was filled with my high pitch scream. It echoed off the walls as I exploded. My body shuddered with spasms of a hot, wrenching ecstasy. I nearly tore a chunk of wood from the desk with my claws. I twisted in overwhelming sensation and gyrated my hips as the waves of my orgasm spilled all over me. I thought I was going to faint from the intensity of the feelings that gripped my being.

It could have been two minutes, but it felt like all the world had been lost for eternity the second I came. Another minute passed for me to recover from the shameful bliss. When my breath returned, I started to get up again.

Looking down between my legs, my juices made a gooey string as Alex pulled her fingers out of me. She got off and stepped back, fished out her white hankie from her hip pocket and wiped my juices off her hand. Alex smirked, looking as if she had just done some petty things on me.

"I hope I get my message across this time," she said, throwing the hankie to the floor. I stared at her with my mouth hanging open. Extreme humiliation got the best of my speech.

I got off the table and smoothed my clothes back in place. Then with one last glare at Alex, I whizzed out of the room and slipped through the door. The hurt could no longer describe how I felt right now. This burn was something that could only be quenched by a sweet revenge. Walking down the hall, I still couldn't shake the anger off my shoulders.

"Don't blame me, Alex," I muttered under my breath. "You make me do this."

CHAPTER 38

Heading back into my room, I pushed open the double doors so hard, the force rattled the hinges. My mind kept drifting back to the frustrating moment with Alex. It lasted about ten minutes. Ten minutes of frantic lustful disgrace and she had already engraved an eternal pain in my gut.

I found Roza sitting on the bed with a shocked expression. She stood up and backed away, looking as if she was trying to blend in with the furniture. I had forgotten to dismiss the girl from my room. For some stupid reason, she didn't leave. So it seemed like now she was in danger of my rising tantrum.

I flashed over to her. She gasped, throwing her hands over her mouth in terror. I guess she must have seen the killer look on my face when I came into the room. Roza understood it was her unlucky day. She stepped back, but I grabbed her by the throat and slammed her frail body on the dressing table. I didn't want to take my anger out on the girl, but I couldn't help it. She happened to be here in the wrong place at the wrong time. I needed to torture someone to get the bad mood out of my system.

With a quick spinning motion, I pinned Roza's innocent freckled face to the table. I could see our reflections in the crystal mirror as I bent her down, spreading her legs apart. Roza cried and begged. Her terrified face was adorable. This fueled my unforgiving rage.

With her backside turned to me, I single-handedly ripped off her panties and let everything fall to the floor. Her pale freckled nakedness was exposed. I spanked and squeezed her behind. How I wished Alex could understand how humiliating it felt. I wasn't going to take Roza in mere sexual lust, but I was going to tortured her.

As my eyes stared at the girl's perched, primed perfect pink flesh, hot saliva flooded my mouth. I was more than ready to feast on my sex slave, but what I intended to give her now was a hell of sensual torture. Licking my lips, I brought two fingers into my mouth then reached down to shove them into Roza. I was more forceful than the way Alex had done to me. The girl's head threw back with her body arched in pain.

Her eyes widened and squeezed shut again to the intense sensation. She clenched her jaw. Her teeth snapped shut to resist the pain. I already went knuckle-deep inside her. The warm walls tensed up around my fingers as she panted, but I kept going. I could hear her miserable whimpers echoed in her throat. Pleading tears trailed down her cheeks. It was a beautiful sight, must be a little painful on her side, but it was a pure pleasure on mine.

Even so, Roza seemed to have high pain tolerance than I thought. It was as if the girl was trained to withstand the harsh physical conditions. I positioned my hips, so I could delve deeper into her tiny depth. She gasped as I reached her electrifying switch and ready to turn it on.

Her lower half started to shiver when she felt me stirring inside her sex pot. I could see her eyes rolled back, mouth flung open, her back arched from the table. Those little pink nipples almost poked through her white shirt. It was a picture of sexual awakening.

But for some reason, I wish I had started nicely with her. Roza had this kind of innocent look that made me want to do naughty things to her longer. I leaned myself over and reached my free hand to her yielding breasts, squeezing them.

I tugged at her hardened nipples to my heart's content. My face nuzzled her neck, nipping away at her blushed cheek.

Roza's fingernails clawed to the table as I thrust my hand into her sweet drooling honey hive. She yelped each time the soaring pleasure coursed through her body. My fingertips faintly brushed over her sensitive button. I wiggled them a bit just to give her a killing tingling.

Sure enough, Roza's hips shuddered with a pelvic sensation. Her breath and heartbeat quickened. And nothing was more exciting than seeing a girl's nirvana began to drip milky nectar down her rosy sex. The scent of Roza's arousal was pure aromatic. I had always wondered why Alex was crazy about her human toy.

Now I understood.

"Are you ready to come for me, slave girl?" I whispered as I was slowly dragging her to the edge of never-ending bliss. "I'll make you come harder than any known species in their mating season. You will cry, you will beg, but you will never want me to end. Brace yourself for it, young lady. It can be your last cry of ecstasy."

As if to prove my point, Roza's body began rippling and shuddering. Her shaking thighs were soaking wet as she could no longer muffle her own orgasmic wailing. My hand kept sliding inside her warm walls, sinking deeper into her sopping girlhood. I felt her pleasurable spot heating up, going on red alert as she was nearing her climax. Her body tensed as the ripples of frenzy orgasmic waves washed over her.

Soon, her moan became a little louder. It looked like her entire body was gripped with a burning ecstasy. Every touch sent a new tide of powerful bliss through her shaking frame. She was helpless as I was with Alex a moment ago. I wanted someone to suffer like me, to make them feel the bitter-sweet agony I had gone through.

Roza was ready to pass out from the blissful eruption I was causing inside her body. Every part of her was shaking, completely lost in a state of blissful havoc. I continued to push her over the edge until a flood of her warm juices ran down from between her spread thighs. It dripped onto the wooden table.

That was when I realized her orgasmic world was successfully blown apart. Roza let out an animal-like howl. Her voice echoed up the palace ceiling. Every muscle in her body jerked with jolts of intense sensation. Her body kept quivering with unimaginable pleasure. Then her knees gave away.

Roza's body went limp on the table. I thought she had passed out, but I heard her faint short-intake breathe continued. Quite a strong little thing indeed, I thought and flipped the girl over to face me again. She was panting, barely conscious after the long-lasting eruptions. I brought down my face to hers, staring at her dazed green eyes.

"You know what honey; I have decided that you're no longer fun anymore," I breathed, tracing my extracted fangs over her neck.

"Please, don't kill me," she tried to beg in a weak whisper.

"Sorry sweetheart, but I have to," I said and bared my sharp venomous teeth at her. Surprisingly, Roza seemed to take her death sentence too calmly. She didn't try to escape or cry for mercy as I expected. She kept staring back at me, which made me a bit uncomfortable.

"Kiss me," she finally said.

"What?"

"Kiss me before I die," Roza's eyes bore into mine. I had never thought I would hear this coming out of her. I was caught off guard. It had been a long time since someone would ask me for a kiss.

"Is that your last wish?" I chuckled. "What a naughty slave you are."

Without much hesitation, I crashed my lips into hers. It didn't take long for the kiss to deepen. My tongue started to roam inside her mouth, exploring and licking her swollen lips. I didn't know a simple act of kissing was so powerful. I heard myself moan into Roza's parted lips. I was being carried away by her innocent kiss that I didn't notice one of her legs raised up to my waist. I thought she was being brave and tried a seductive method on me. But then my eyes caught a glimpse of our reflection in the mirror.

Roza's hand was holding a shiny curved blade, about twelve inches long. Its gleam reflected against the sunlight. The girl made a lightning strike at me. Her razor-sharp knife aimed directly at my throat, attempting to slit it out. But I pulled away just in time and grabbed her wrist, twisting the knife out of her hand.

"What the..." I stared at the girl as my hand went back to her throat.

"Go to hell, you bloodsucker!" Roza snarled back.

I looked at her long curved blade and then back at the innocent-looking human Roza again.

"A hunter?"

CHAPTER 39

AVERY

I brushed the tips of my fingers over the smooth black piano, then lifted open the lid and pressed on a tiny white key. The sharp high-pitch note resonated across the empty room. But even after the sound ceased, my heart still buzzed with unspeakable torment. Misery held me down like an anchor and drowned me deeper than the ocean. Painful tears started to sting my eyes as I stared at the elegant piano again.

How could it not be clearer to me? Had I been sleepwalking the whole time? Alex loved me. She loved me more than I could imagine, but maybe there was a clog in my brain that made me unable to grasp the notion. And now it was too late. I let my own stubbornness and ignorance thickened like a fog around my heart. And now it was too late to wipe it away. It was too late to clear my eyes from it.

"I'm sorry Alex," I whispered, feeling the inside of my throat turn raw. "I'm sorry that I can't love you the way you love me. I know this will kill you, but I have to. I'm so sorry."

Wiping the tears from my cheeks, I closed the piano lid again and walked out of the room. I didn't want to look back at anything in the place, because if I did, it would remind me of the time we had spent together. I would never be able to get out. It was for the best. Alex and I didn't belong together.

I was Anastasia's from the start. We loved each other, it was meant to be, and I was doing the right thing.

"Thanks for the memories," I said as I closed the grand oak door then gathered myself back and ran as fast as I could. I had to run before the pain could catch up to me.

Along the corridors and down the hall, I ran back to the east wing of the mansion. I reached Anastasia's chamber again. When I burst into her room, I called her name once and twice. My heart pounded in my chest. The moment was so overwhelming. My hands trembled at my sides. I got to find Ana quick or everything wouldn't be the same. A moment later, I found her standing by an unfinished painting.

"Anastasia!" I cried. And when she finally turned around, I flew right into her arms. She was a bit surprised at first, but she held me back. I hugged her angelic frame tighter, breathing in the sweet fragrant scent of her smooth skin. My cheek brushed over her shoulder with longing. I held her tightly as if I couldn't be close enough to her.

"Are you alright, baby?" she cooed in my ear, smoothing my hair down my back. For a moment, I couldn't speak. Words failed me. Why was it too hard to say it? Say what you have to, damn it! I squeezed my eyes shut and let out a whining sound.

"Hey hey...shhh...what is it, love? Tell me what's wrong?" Ana pulled me away as she heard me sobbing. Her golden eyes stared warily at my face.

"Ana..." I began in a choking voice. "I've decided..."

"You what?" she asked, sounding quite concerned rather than surprised.

"It's you, Anastasia," I uttered as clear as I could. "I want you. I want to be with you and no one else. I love you."

I threw my arms around her again, but my feet went wobbly as if it had taken every ounce of my strength to declare this. Anastasia caught me with her strong arms. But she seemed speechless at this unexpected situation.

"Hold me, Anastasia, please," I whispered against her neck, "Don't let me go. Don't let it get to me."

"Don't let what?" she asked.

"I don't know, I don't know, I don't know!" I cried like a crazy person and buried my face into her even more.

"Alright, alright...sweetheart, I won't let you go, I promise," Ana was desperate to calm me down. She rubbed my back.

After what seemed like a long while, we pulled away. When my breath became normal again, Anastasia took my hand to a white couch by the French window. She sat down and pulled me to her lap. I curled up into her body and rested my forehead on her shoulder. My eyes kept staring at the tiny white pattern on the hem of her satin dress. Ana stroked my cheek as I was lost in my own world.

"Avery, I could hear the pain in your voice," Anastasia said. "You have no idea how much that makes my heart ache."

"You're not happy to be with me?" I asked.

"Yes I am," she said. "I'm just wondering..."

Oh Anastasia, shut up! I thought. You know me too well, it scares me.

"Please, just don't," I said, bringing my index finger to her lips. "Just let me have you. You're perfect for me. I want no one but you."

In a desperate attempt to convince her, I smashed my lips into hers, kissing Anastasia's moist scented lips with mine. She responded slowly and timidly, but I kept forcing her to kiss me back until she gave in. Anastasia's divine face broke into a smile.

I was doing the right thing.

CHAPTER 40

NIKOL

Roza sat on the floor by the comfy sofa with her arms wrapped around her knees. Her green eyes kept staring at me as I paced back and forth, swinging her twelve-inch blade in my hand. If there was a hunter on the loose inside the Palace, there would be more of them roaming around the Kremlin Walls. Roza must have been captured by our army and then got enslaved. She managed to keep her cover. I figured if she were a skilled hunter, I would have been dead by now. Roza was still too young and too nervous for the task.

I stopped and stared at the girl again. She might not seem much for now, but I knew deep down that this innocent human could be my secret weapon to get back at Alex. If I could convince her to bring out her clan, it would be easy to use the hunters as my puppet too. I never thought I would have to rely on my backup plan, but Alex was the only stumbling block I had to toss aside. There was no way I was going to spend the rest of my eternity being the underdog. Not anymore, not to Alexandra Romanov.

"So you're a hunter, huh?" I said, arching my eyebrow in disbelief. "Who sent you here?"

"Just kill me already," Roza hissed through her teeth. Her bright green eyes gazed at me with hatred. I knew hunters had their code of conducts, so I wasn't going to spend my energy interrogating her either.

Walking toward the girl again, I grabbed her by the throat and stood her up to face me.

"Let me tell you something, honey," I said and brought the sharp blade to her soft freckled cheek. I pressed the edge against her skin a little. Roza winced in my hand. "I can kill you with just a snap of my fingers, in any way I want at any time I want. But I figure that you can do something for the greater good, so I will give you a chance to live up to it."

"What do you mean?" Roza asked through her tight throat. I released her from my hand. She dropped back on the couch and coughed.

"Just so you know, I wasn't your real target, young lady. If you and your hunters join force with me..." I said and threw the knife down the table. The sharp curved blade sunk half way through the thick wood. "We all will be freed from this excruciating hell together."

Roza stared at the knife wide eyes and then turned her face back at me. I reached my hand out and cupped her chin. My face hovered over hers as I stared deep into her green eyes.

"Roza, you're a smart girl, do you know you can be the one to bring the downfall to the Russian empire?"

"You think I'm going to believe that?" she said with a grimace.

"I understand how miserable your people feel. I was human once," I said. "Seeing you being enslaved like animals just breaks my heart."

"You could have fooled me," Roza said.

I let out a laugh.

"Alright, so what about this?" I said. "If you don't do as I say, you will die a horrible, painful death, not to mention a worthless one. Just think about it, sweetie. You've got nothing else to lose."

"How can I know whether you will turn against us?" she said.

"Silly girl, I was from the Bolshevik party. You think I forget my enemy?" I pretended to say. Roza's eyes flicked as if she was molding the idea inside her young naive mind.

"And what do you want me to do?"

I beamed at the girl.

"Tell your hunters that if they follow my plan, they can have the imperial princess—first in line to the Russian throne. How about that?"

"You mean Grand Duchess Alexandra?" Roza said. I could see her eyes lighted up with nervousness and excitement.

"Exactly." I smiled.

It didn't take me long to find the good old starets man. He was in his office as the guards had told me. Rasputin had just returned from one of the raids he had ordered. The high-profile attacks from the hunters seemed to have multiplied in the last few days. No wonder why the man looked stressed when I entered his room.

"Long day?" I asked, closing the office door behind me and leaned against it. Rasputin jumped in his chair at the sound of my voice.

"What are you doing here?"

"Let me get to the point," I said and walked to his table. Putting my hands on the desktop, I leaned myself forward him. Rasputin stared at me with his mouth flung open. I knew he was trying so hard not to look at the area of my chest.

"I know you've been a good friend to the Czar family," I started. "You gained their respect from your so-called rituals and whatnot, but guess what? You were still the reason why the Bolsheviks dethroned the Czar."

"What are you talking about?"

"What I'm saying is that no matter how hard you try to work for the Grand Duchess, it's still useless," I said. "She will never forget the misfortune you brought to her family."

"That's not true!" Rasputin stood up, his nostrils flared with rising anger.

"Relax," I said and floated to his side. "It's not like we can ignore the fact that you had caused quite a rumor with former Czarina. And we all know Alex loved her mother. Even I don't know whether your love affair was true or not, it had already left a black spot on your name. No one is going to trust you. Admit it, Rasputin, you and I are the dirt in Alexandra's eyes."

"Why do you bring this up? What do you want?" Rasputin was breathing hard now. His violet eyes bore into mine. I knew I had worked him up pretty bad, it amused me.

"I have a plan for you," I whispered, leaning my face toward him.

"A plan?"

"I know it sounds bad and it is," I said with a small giggle. "You can never be great and powerful if someone's already at the top. I know you want power. I just want my freedom back. How about you sit here and do absolutely nothing while I shake my stick and get our wishes granted?"

"Holy sh—" the starets cried as his brain started to work around the scheme, "Don't tell me you want to..."

"Yes, that's what I want to do, and you're now a part of the plan."

Rasputin stumbled backward and then slumped himself down on his chair again. It looked as if the shock was too heavy for him to handle.

"You have no idea what you're up against, Nikol," He spoke in a trembling voice.

"Of course, I'm not that stupid to do the job myself, Rasputin," I said, rolling my eyes at him. "No one can even know that it's us. Think about it."

"How could that be possible?"

"Just bring the tiger out of the cave," I said with an alluring smile, "The hunters will take care of the rest."

I reached my hand out and patted him on the cheek before leaving the room.

CHAPTER 41

ANASTASIA

"Long time no see. Are you up for a good ride today, Stardust?" I said to my thoroughbred horse as I stepped in the barn, a bag of pieces of apple in my hand. Stardust's cotton white coat shone like a puffy morning cloud. The mare hung her head over her stall door and let out an eager whinny in response. Her white mane flowed like raw silk. I reached up to pat her strong shoulder. Stardust's ears twitched in delight as I motioned to our human stable boys to take the horse out.

The white mare shook her powerful neck as she walked into a stream of spring sunshine. I took the reins from the stable boy and fed some more apple pieces to the horse.

"You want to get out and go as much as I do, don't you?" I adjusted the saddle on Stardust's back and fastened the throat latch. Then I slipped on my helmet and buckled it up, not that I needed protection. It was an old habit. Before I led my horse outside, my eyes glanced at an enormous coal-black stallion at the end of the stable. It was Alex's favorite horse, Thunderstorm. The horse was all clipped and groomed; his whole body glowed with a coppery shine. In fact, Thunderstorm was even faster than Stardust and much stronger. But now the animal just hung his head low over the stall door, his sad eyes looked at me. I felt sorry for

Thunderstorm. He was probably missing his mistress. I turned my head back and tried not to think about Alex.

Once we were out of the barn, I swung onto Stardust's back, taking a deep breath of the fresh morning air. Stardust's impatient hooves pawed on the ground.

"Let's go for a warm-up ride, shall we?" I said and pressed the heels of my riding boots against the horse's sides. Stardust began to gallop forward.

I had left a note for Avery to wait for me at the backyard of the mansion. It was still early and I didn't want to wake her at this hour. But Avery was already there. She was sitting on a loveseat inside the cabana. The silky curtains flicked against the breeze around her. She rose up from the seat when she saw me approaching.

Avery was in her beautiful high-waisted wool dress, which I got for her. Her brown hair braided down one side to match a Byzantine design on the flowing fabric. Her face lighted up. I smiled back at her and then stopped the horse.

"Oh my goodness, Anastasia," she gasped as she eyed the white horse. She walked toward us but then stopped a few steps away. It was more like she didn't want to startle Stardust. I got off the horse and walked toward her and took off my riding helmet.

"Good morning, beautiful," I said, taking her lovely hand in mine and bowed down to kiss it. Avery giggled at my action. I smiled and slid my hands around her waist and pulled her delicate body against mine. Her youthful cheeks blushed crimson.

"You look like you come straight out of a fairy tale," Avery said. She traced her lovely fingers over a row of gold buttons of my white gothic long-tail coat, my favorite riding coat.

"I could say the same thing to you," I said.

Avery giggled and twirled my long wavy blonde hair around with her fingers.

"I don't know whether to call you beautiful or handsome, Anastasia."

"You can call me both," I said with a smirk.

"How vain!" she teased back.

I burst out laughing.

"Right, I can be your princess, and you can be my Cinderella," I said. "Now let me taste those sweet lips before midnight comes."

And I pressed my lips against hers. She took my face in her hands and deepened our kiss. Spring sunlight broke through the clouds and bathed us with its golden warmth.

We would have kissed forever if it wasn't for a snorting sound from Stardust. We broke off and turned ourselves to look at my horse. Stardust shook her horsehair and snorted some more. Avery and I laughed. She walked slowly towards Stardust. I was relieved that Avery wasn't afraid of horses. The creature seemed to welcome her with calmness. Avery reached her hand out and gave a gentle rub on Stardust's white snout.

"She's beautiful," Avery said, "so white and huge like a unicorn!"

I laughed again.

"Her name is Stardust," I told her, coming to stand by her side. "She's a thoroughbred racehorse. Today, Stardust will bring us to places you have never been. Are you ready for a ride with us?"

Avery smiled and nodded. I kissed her lips one more time before proceeding to help her get on the horse's back. I made sure the seat was steady and comfortable for Avery before I got myself up behind her too.

"Ready?" I asked and Avery nodded, looking excited of the feeling of being on a horse.

Gripping the reins, I was also holding her in my arms. Our cheeks brushed faintly against each other. I couldn't stop myself from smiling. Then I tugged the reins, wheeling Stardust around. We headed out of the backyard, going up the small hill then further to the wood.

As we finally got out of the woodland again, Stardust took us into a wide beautiful meadow. Wildflowers of all kinds blossomed everywhere. I made Stardust gallop through the tall green grass and chased little birds just for the thrill of it. Avery laughed and screamed in joy, and she was my joy herself. We rode like that through cold wind and the sunshine. I felt so alive.

Stardust led us to a small creek with clear water running and we decided to take a rest around there. I helped Avery off the horse then let Stardust free to munch on the fresh grass.

Avery and I walked hand in hand up toward a big chestnut tree. She looked around the field with sparkling eyes.

"It's so beautiful here," she breathed. "A small creek, a mountain view and a meadow full of flowers, it's even beautiful than the garden."

"The garden?" I asked. Avery looked at me and then she shook her head.

"Let's rest here," she said instead.

I nodded, and we sat down on the soft green grass under the tree. I gave a peck on Avery's cheek again before rolling onto my back and resting my head on her lap. She giggled and brought her palm to my cheek. I played with her long braided hair and simply enjoyed each other's company.

"I don't want this moment to end," I said later, "If I could stop the sun from setting, I would. I want to stay like this with you. It feels like being in heaven. You make everything even more beautiful than it is."

"You're exaggerating." Avery smiled, stroking my cheek with her thumb.

"I'm not. I do want to stay like this with you forever."

"Forever is not in my time zone, you know," she pointed out.

I looked up into her dark brown eyes. She had grown slowly into a beautiful woman, no longer an innocent teenager I had seen many months ago. Then I moved myself over to make room for Avery and motioned for her to sit down next to me. I pulled her body in my arms, resting her head on my chest and rubbed her back. Neither of us spoke again. We both looked at the high blue sky together.

"Aren't you afraid?" I said again.

"Of what?"

"Of having to be with me for a very long time?"

"No," she said without a pause. "I hope I can live to be a hundred year like you." And we both broke out giggling.

"Then I'll be over two centuries old."

"Except that you don't look the part," Avery added. I laughed again and kissed her on the top of her head. Avery wrapped her arm around me and I tightened my grip around her. If possible, I just wanted to have her close to me at all time.

"Someday I will die, you know," Avery suddenly said, "unless—"

"I still don't want to change anything about you," I interrupted her.

"So you're afraid then?"

I thought of it for a moment before I spoke.

"Yes, I am."

"Why?" Avery's head turned, and she looked at me with a deep frown. Her eyes stirred with confusion. "You think I will end up like Nikol?"

"No, you are you. That's entirely different," I told her. "I'm scared because you mean to me more than anything. You are everything I think about. Everything I've ever wanted. But you don't have to pick a flower because you love it."

"The flower will die anyway," she said.

"Yes, but not so soon."

"Anastasia, why are you talking like that?" Avery said.

"I just want to let you know that you deserve something better. You give me so much, but you forget yourself." I said, looking back at her. "Even it burns my heart to picture you with someone else, I have to admit that sometimes love is about letting go. I wish I had realized that earlier. Alex did."

"Why does everybody always keep saying that to me?" She cried and sat up, crystal tears welled up in her eyes.

"Avery, have you ever stopped to think, that what if I'm not the right person for you?" I said as we stared at each other. "What if it hasn't always been me, but Alex you've been in love with? You chose to be with me, but your heart is in Russia. I could feel the tug of your pain every time the thought of Alex crossed. You saw her first, and not me."

"But I didn't love her then, I loved you, and I still do now."

"I know," I said. "Alex didn't realize she fell in love with you either. You both are quite the same. You're both deeply in love with each other, yet unable to understand your own hearts."

"Anastasia, please!" Avery cried, covering her ears and turning her face away from me. "I don't want to hear it anymore." I looked at her as she wrapped her arms around her knees and began to cry. How I wished she knew I would do anything to kiss the tears away from her face.

"Avery." I moved over to her and pulled her body into my arms again. "I want you to be happy."

"I'm already happy with you, Anastasia," she insisted in a choking voice. She turned around to wrap her arms around my neck. I held her with a sigh and stroked her hair to calm her down.

"Imagine if you were happy with the wrong person, how happy would you be with the right one?" I said.

"Please stop, Anastasia, it hurts," Avery pleaded in tears. Her whole body shook, her breath hitched. I winced at the same pain inside my chest. A small tear rolled down my cheek as I kept holding her.

"I'm so sorry Avery, I love you too much, I have to let you go," I whispered. Avery pressed her face against me and sobbed even harder. In that moment, I realized there was nothing left but two broken hearts.

CHAPTER 42

NIKOL

The door creaked and Roza's petite form stepped inside. I rushed over to her and pushed the door shut again. I grabbed Roza by the wrist and led her back into the room.

"Did anyone see you?" I asked in a low voice.

"No," she said. "I was alone."

"Good." I nodded in relief. "Now tell me what your hunters said about my plan."

"Well, it was hard to convince them, but they finally agreed," Roza replied. "I told them what you had told me. When everything comes to an end, you will set our people free. We only wait for your turn."

I looked at Roza, somehow I felt bad for this young girl. It didn't take much for me to twist her mortal mind. Did she actually think I would help them, humans?

"Don't worry about it," I said with a satisfied smile. "The time will come."

"What about the other Romanov?"

"Huh?"

"Grand Duchess Anastasiya, another imperial princess, remember?" Roza said, sounding as if she was scolding me. I didn't forget about Ana. After I was through with Alex, she would the new heiress of Russia. Of course, that was exactly what I wanted. But I wouldn't tell Roza that. She had no part in this one.

"Ah," I breathed, pretending to go along with her. "Anastasia won't be much of a problem to us. The princess doesn't care about the politics. Besides she will be exiled from Russia anyway."

In fact, I was more excited to have Anastasia back in my hand. I know I would have to forgive my young duchess for losing her mind over a slave girl. Once I crossed that human girl out of the equation, Anastasia would never dare to escape me ever again. I would make her mine, and we would rule the world together.

"Are you sure we can take them down?" Roza asked.

"As long as your side doesn't mess up," I said. "But I trust your people."

"You don't look like the trusting type or the trustworthy one," she said, eyeing me in a total judging way. I fought the urge to snap my teeth at her. This little hunter girl was starting to get on my last civilized nerve, but I tried not to let it show. Roza didn't know the rest of my plan. After the hunters take care of Alex, they would put themselves right into another trap. I had already plotted the whole scheme with Rasputin. One stone kills two birds, how brilliant is that? And when Russia finally falls into my hand, no one could tell me what to do. I will get Anastasia and the empire all to myself. And if anything goes wrong, Rasputin will be the perfect figure for me to frame for this treachery.

This should wipe my hands clean off this mess.

Simple as that.

"Roza," I said, tugging a strand of hair behind her ear. My charm never failed to seduce a girl like her. "This is for our own good. Something great is going to happen for you and me, you can't deny that. So why don't we put our hatred aside and celebrate our future victory together now?"

Roza's eyes lighted up a little. Then her cheeks blushed. I realized our bodies were already touching. Her small but adorable looking body drew me in like a magnet. My breasts pushed up against hers. Regardless of her attempt to kill me the other day, I sort of enjoyed having the girl with me again, though.

Looking into her eyes, I ran my fingers over Roza's freckled cheek and raised her chin up to me. I knew I wanted to devour Roza one more time before she got what she deserved. My other hand reached out to those supple breasts of hers.

"Don't you do that to me again," Roza hissed, swatting my hand away. "I'm not going to be your sex object anymore."

"Oh is that so? But you're my partner in crime now, and that is kind of the same thing," I said. My hands gripped her around the waist, pulling her body forcefully against mine.

"I don't want it that way," Roza's hands tried to push at my shoulders, but I tightened my grip around her body. She yelped.

"I can break your ribs, Roza, don't piss me off this time," I said, looking squarely into her green eyes. She flinched and bit her lips. What did she think she would get from all this protesting? Stupid girl, she would still end up giving herself over to me. The taste of being with a hunter was quite alluring after all.

Roza glared hard at my face, but she stopped struggling and let me push her to the wall. I brought my nose closer to her neck. My cold breath caused goose bumps on her skin.

"You're the most horrible vampire I've ever seen, you should know that," Roza spat.

"Of course, not to mention twisted and irresistible," I said with a low snicker, enjoying the blush on her freckled cheeks.

"But whatever you say, don't come unless I tell you to, huntress."

At the very magical word, her body melted into my arms. It was surprising how this girl still continued to amuse me. I leaned down to nuzzle her neck, tracing my tongue over her exposed skin. My hands wound up inside her skirt, frantically squeezing around her tight bum. Roza gasped at my ravenous touch over her skin. I knew just how she liked it.

I snaked my hand down and slipped it inside her cotton panties. Roza threw her head back and bit her bottom lip. I lifted her thigh up to my waist and continued to stroke the wet sensitivity between her legs. The little huntress started whimpering in my ear.

The sound of her pleasurable moans was what I needed to hear. Shredding off her white blouse, I buried my face into her soft supple bouncing breasts. My lips and tongue feasted on her hardened nipples. I teethed them until she yelped in pleasure.

I eased down Roza's panties and started tracing my fingers over her lovely flaps. She was so wet.

"Oh, my, who's the excited one now?" I purred into her ear.

But Roza was beyond caring now. Her fingers ran through my hair, pulling my head to her arching breasts for more suckle. I was more than happy to give the service. My palm was soaked with her sweetness. Every now and then Roza would try to push her hips into me. This not-so-innocent girl was desperate for me to claim her again. I stroked her sensitive rosebud harder, causing her to let loose some more of her juices. Her bright green eyes flashed with the heat of pleading lust. But this was just a quick warm up before the main course.

Parting her legs even farther, I trailed kisses down from her breasts and to her flat stomach then right to her secret nest. I placed one of her legs over my shoulder and leaned down until my face was inches away from her feminine flesh. With steady fingers, I stretched open her raw sex canal and inhaled her sweet scent. Roza was trembling with excitement. Her inner thighs glistened with her own juices. I knew she was ready for any special treatment she was about to receive from me, and I wasn't going to make her wet for long.

I started attacking her femininity, tongue-wrestling with her heated pearl. My fingers poked gently into her dripping flesh, stroking her swelling walls until I was rewarded with loud whimpers. After a while, Roza couldn't resist any longer. Her sweet greedy sex was already twitching and lubricating in readiness. It was quite fun and arousing to be adventurous with Roza. I got to explore her body's triggers and play around like she was my supple sex doll.

I ran my skillful tongue up and down her soaked canyon, tickling over her lovely flower. With my mischievous fingers joining the tease, Roza's heartbeat went wild. I licked the juices from within. I tasted her salty nectar earnestly, torturing the girl with more burning lust. The girl's eyes got teary from a tingling sensation. Her jaw dropped as she looked down at the hateful enemy between her legs.

At last, I slipped my glistened fingers inside her. I came back up to see the shell-shocked girl ready for a wild ride. My hand lifted Roza's knee again, spreading her wider open for a deep penetrative sex I was going to give her. I kept delving into her soft cave until she threw her arms around my body and moaned out of sheer sexual delight. She clung to my shoulders like a scared koala in a hurricane.

"How do you like that, my little hunter?" I chuckled and knocked her up a little with my fingers buried inside her walls. Roza wailed in the sweetest wanton tone I'd ever heard. I laughed, feeling her weakest spot already pleading for my mercy. I did it again and again until she clawed on my skin and screamed.

"Please please...I can't...I can't..." Roza begged, breathless.

"Just hold on, the first big surprise is coming," I whispered and brought my lips to hers. I kept thrusting my hungry tongue down her throat, almost choking her with my deep and hard kiss.

My fingers began easing in and out of Roza's wet femininity. I pressed and rubbed her heated bud. It sent sparks of sensual pleasure over Roza's orgasmic world. She moaned, but the sound was muffled against my mouth as I was still tonguing around her throat. She tried to escape for some intakes of air, but I always got her back for more lip-locking. Until the girl's breath became extremely loud and uneven, I realized she was going to cum in no time. Her entrance started twitching and closing in.

"No, no, not yet, try to hold it back....as long as you can," I advised. "I promise it will worth it."

Roza did try, but her eyes fluttered and rolled back when the tingling sensation started mounting up inside her rocking form. I managed to get the girl to kiss me again, yet I still kept the rhythm steady and direct inside her orgasmic tunnel. Drawing more and more clear juices out of her entrance, I started bringing Roza to the edge for good.

After a long wild ride, her world finally stopped orbiting. The powerful explosion pushed her headlong into a wormhole of the ecstatic universe. Roza's body shook and shuddered as she came with a loud wail. After she swam through waves after waves of climaxing shocks, it was over. The girl looked helpless and weightless.

She collapsed into my arms, panting like a baby rabbit from exhaustion. I smiled, smoothing her hair as I looked down at the still-shuddering girl in my hands.

"Told you, great sex comes to those who wait," I said then laughed at my own joke. "So are you ready for the second big surprise, young lady?" When the word sunk in, Roza lifted her head to stare at me blankly.

"The second big surprise? What...what does it mean?"

I didn't answer her. My hands gripped her firmly by the shoulders and pushed her body back against the wall again. Roza looked terrified as she stared at my face, now that I looked murderous. I pulled my lips back over my white teeth. The throbbing feeling around my jaw was begging me to squeeze the fangs out. Roza immediately fought back, but I was quicker and already pinned her hands to the wall.

"A sweet happy ending of you and me, isn't it?" I said through my elongated canines. Then with a flash, I lunged myself forward, aiming right at her delicate throat. My dagger-shaped teeth broke through the soft layer of Roza's pale skin. They buried deep into her main vessel easily. Roza screamed from the burning pain. My arms tightened around her body, locking the girl in a death-like grip. No matter how hard Roza fought, I still continued sucking on her fresh delicious blood. I was feeding off her essence with hungry growls rising from the pit of my stomach. Her incredible taste traveled down my throat, energizing me like sweet ambrosia. The more I drank, the thirstier I became.

Roza's body went limp in my hands, her head lulled on my shoulder. That was when I realized the huntress was finally lifeless.

CHAPTER 43

ALEXANDRA

I stood looking at the Moskva River through the window. Saint Basil's Cathedral and the Red Square were in my view to the east. I could see Alexander Garden sprawled out from the west side. But everything felt so empty. Moscow was empty and cold and sad. Russia, Window to the West, was now a depressing sight.

But it amazed me how I could still survive without Avery up to this point. It hurt every freaking night. I didn't know how long I could live with this. As if my heart would need a fortress stronger than Kremlin to keep it inside Russia. My heart knew no distance or time, all it was beating for was to be with my loved one. I missed the dizzying happiness with her. I missed her soft skin, her delicious lips, her fragrant scent.

But then the undeniable truth hit me. I didn't deserve Avery. She didn't love me. I had hurt her. She was in love with Anastasia. My sister was perfect for her. Why would Avery choose someone like me? All these painful thoughts stirred up a sharp sting so real that I had to clutch my chest with a gasp.

There was a knock on the door. I collected myself, taking a deep breath before turning around.

"Your highness," Rasputin's voice spoke as he entered the room. "It's already time."

I sighed before stepping away from the city view. It was an annual meeting of the Royal Council. It was mostly about the boring law enforcement and boring banquet afterward. I didn't want to go, but I had to represent Russia at the table. Rasputin just informed me about it last night. I thought it wouldn't start until sometimes later.

"Alright, let's go," I said, but before we walked out of the room. Rasputin reached out his hand to stop me.

"Grand Duchess," he said with an uneasy tone.

"You have something to say?"

"I...I...er..." he started, "I mean...nothing, your highness."

But his face looked paler than usual.

"You don't look well," I said. "That's alright. You don't have to go with me this time."

Rasputin looked at me, somewhat shocked, but then he nodded.

A moment later, as we were in the Portrait Hall, I remembered something.

"Where's Nikol?" I asked Rasputin.

"I'm not aware of that, your highness," he said, looking a bit fidget. "But why do you ask?"

"I haven't seen her much these days," I said with a frown. "That's odd."

With a snap decision, I decided to check on her. The guards posted around her chamber stiffened when they saw me approaching. But after they pushed the doors of her room open, there was no Nikol there.

"Where is she?" I asked, stepping out again to look at the guards. Rasputin almost flinched under my curious stare. I wondered what was wrong with him today.

"Who are you looking for? Me?" Nikol appeared from the other side of the hall. She walked up to us and crossed her arms.

"Where have you been, Nikol?" I said.

"Oh now you remember I exist," she said.

"Knock it off," I hissed, stepping closer to her. "I don't want anything to do with you either. But you have to come to the council meeting with me."

"What?" Nikol's voice squeaked. "Why do I have to go?"

"Because I said so," I said. "You have five minutes to get ready. Don't waste my time."

Nikol glared at me. Then her eyes instinctively gazed at Rasputin. It was so quick, you could have missed it, but something in her eyes seemed to tickle my gut.

"What is it?" I asked, looking between her and Rasputin.

"Nothing," she said and then she turned away. There was this strange aura around her. But I still had difficulty framing it.

A while later we were in the car. Nikol sat next to me. She didn't talk or tried anything stupid with me, which was good, but I couldn't seem to get her silence this time. It made me a little uncomfortable.

The black limousines and SUV cars whizzed out of the palace and across the Red Square. I looked through the window until we reached one of the city gates. The sky was darkening.

"Wait, why are we heading here?" I asked the driver. Then I noticed the quiet atmosphere of the area. Building and streets looked abandoned. It was the east gate of Moscow, the furthest outskirt of the city. "Why is there no one guarding this entrance?"

"Rasputin ordered them to leave," Nikol spoke for the first time without looking at me.

"How do you know he did that?" I turned my head to her.

"Because I told him to," she said, turning to look at me with her deep violet eyes.

I was about to ask her for clarity, but then I heard an explosion from behind our car. The shock wave cracked our bulletproof windows. My eardrums almost split at the sound. I turned around to find two of our SUV cars were ablaze.

"The hunters!" one of the royal guards yelled. "We're under attack!" Our soldiers rushed out of their cars, but they got shot from all directions and collapsed to ground one by one. Then a long metal-tipped arrow struck through the window on my side. Shards of glass flew all over the seat.

"Damn it!" I hissed and pushed open the door to get out. The hunters were hiding in every corner of the empty streets and tall buildings. Everywhere I turned; it was raging with chaotic screaming and running. Then ropes unrolled from the walls and a dozen of hunters slid through them.

They were armed with crossbows and long curved blades. Once their feet reached the ground, arrows flew everywhere. The guards tried to counter attack but most of them got shot in the chest. The vampires were faster and stronger, but the hunters were well-trained. It was going to be a severe bloodbath without a doubt.

I turned back to the car again, but Nikol was gone. She was probably hiding her behind from all sorts of harm. I already imagined her watching from a safe distance by now—that coward.

"Your highness!" a guard came stumbling toward me, "You can't stay here. There are too many of them."

An arrow burst through his chest from behind. The guard fell to the ground in front of me. That's when I saw a hunter wearing a white fur coat with the hood on. He stood with his crossbow pointing at me.

"You don't want to do that," I said to him.

But he still pulled the trigger. The arrow shot out. I could see its tip sailing straight at me, but I dodged it just in time. It hit one of the cars instead. Except I didn't know it had an explosive tip. And a roar of ear-splitting blast erupted only ten feet away from me. A mushroom of red flame burst out. The shock wave hurled me to the ground, causing the world to spin for a moment.

I sat up and saw black smoke emitting to the air. Getting on my feet again, I saw two other hunters appeared. They drew out their shining hatchets and curved blades from their backs. One of them threw a hatchet at me. I did a back-flip, missing the weapon barely an inch. The other lunged forward, but I welcomed him with a kick to the chest. He went airborne and broke through a window shop.

When the last one came at me, one of the royal guards took care of him. Then the frenzy biting and stabbing started between them. I didn't wait to see who died first and flashed over to another hunter. I slammed him against the car hard. Then I rushed back to the one who tried to shoot me, grabbing him by the throat.

"Get yourself out of here before I tear you apart!" I growled at him through my sharp teeth. He was struggling like a child against my iron grip. Then I heard a soft whinny sound. I pulled the hoodie off and realized the hunter was just a girl. She had those big brown eyes and dark brown hair flowing down her white fur coat. I stared at the girl. I could have snapped her little neck easily, but I didn't. She was about Avery's age.

I was distracted until a sharp pain burst in my body. Someone stabbed me in the back. My anguish cry filled the air. The person was quite strong for a hunter. I pushed the human girl to the ground. She stared back at me in confusion and then stumbled away. My backstabber wrapped one arm around my neck before pulling the blade out of my body. My eyes widened at the horrible pain. I could feel the blood surging from my open wound.

"Surprise!" Nikol's voice said in a singsong tone.

"Nic...Nikol?"

Before I could process what was going on, she gave me a second hard stab. It sent a wave of shock and dizziness through me. My jaw snapped open in agony. I could feel the hot blood flowing. Then my knees buckled and I fell to the ground. Nikol turned me onto my back. She was already sitting on my stomach, pinning my body down with her entire weight. Then she pointed a shiny curved blade to my throat. My eyes went blur as I lay in the red pool of blood around me.

"That's for what you have done to me, Alexandra," she smiled in my face. "I would love to have the hunters kill you for me, but I figure I should do it myself. So it's now or never."

"Why? Nikol, why are you doing this?"

"You know the answer better than anyone, Alex!" she yelled back. "I'm sick of living under your shadow. With you out of the picture, everything will be mine and only mine! Anastasia and the empire...oh and don't forget, I also get to have your human lover in my hand. But of course, I won't keep her for long, because she'll be sent to hell with you after this."

I could see the madness in her eyes. My back hurt so bad, it paralyzed me on the spot.

"Oh poor Alex," Nikol cooed at me. "I know exactly where to strike, don't worry about it. Evolution moved your heart right here, we all know that don't we?" she traced the curved blade to the middle of my chest. "I promise to get the job done quick and easy, Alex. Just prepare yourself to die."

Nikol raised her hand, aiming the tip of her sharp knife directly at my heart. But when she struck, I caught her hand in mine. She could have run the blade through me if I hadn't stopped her.

"Nikol...don't be stupid," I hissed, struggling against her.

"Shut up!" she snapped her fangs at me. "You can't tell me what to do anymore." With all her strength, Nikol gave one final push that slid the blade through my chest. I felt it piercing into my beating organ. I screamed like never before. The blood spilled out from my wound. The sweet metallic scent clogged my nostril. I felt my stomach churn. My head spun with dizziness. The pain was insane. I gasped and almost passed out, but I tried to bring myself back to consciousness.

"Goodbye Alexandra Romanov," she said with a victorious smile. I bit my lips and summoned all my last strength. I clenched my teeth. She didn't expect this. Then I struck my claw into her body, breaking her chest bone. Her blood splashed on our faces. I grabbed a handful of her living flesh and ripped the heart out. Nikol's mouth flung open as she stared down at me in total shock.

"Surprised?" I said, squeezing her beating heart in my hand. Blood dripped furiously from the hole of her heartless body. Nikol turned as white as chalk. And that's when death had consumed her soul. I managed to push her body off and proceeded to pull the blade from my chest. It felt as worse as getting another stab. My breath quickened. My bleeding heart would never heal. I knew I couldn't survive. I was going to die eventually.

Despite all that, I didn't want to close my eyes. As I was lying on the blood-soaked ground waiting for all my senses to leave my body, I watched the dark clouds drifting away from the blue sky. Patches of light appeared over the earth once again.

"I'm sorry Avery," I whispered into the air, hoping the wind could carry my message thousands mile away from here. "I'm so sorry, I can't go back to you, but I love you, forever and always."

Tears rolled off my eyes. I felt cold and then—nothing.

CHAPTER 44

AVERY

My head rested against Anastasia's back as we were riding Stardust back to the mansion. It was getting colder as twilight began to fade. Anastasia had taken off her white coat and draped it around my shoulders. Stardust's footsteps were the only sound we heard through the wood as neither of us said anything. Of course, there was nothing left to say anymore. Finally, the forest fell to the background, and we got back into the backyard garden at last.

Ana looked over her shoulder and whispered to me, "Are you alright?"

"Mmm..." I gave a weak nod.

"I'm getting off now."

I nodded again and removed my hands from her waist. She gracefully swung herself off Stardust and came to help me. I wrapped my hands around her neck and let myself fall into her waiting arms. The stable boys came to take the white mare back to the barn. But even after Anastasia put me down on my feet, I still didn't let go of her. It felt as if it was for the last time I could do that.

"It's alright," she said, knowing the cause of my gloomy mood.

"I'm sorry," I said in a small voice. "I didn't mean to hurt you that way. I just messed up."

Anastasia stroked my hair and sighed.

"Don't feel sorry for me," she whispered.

"But it's not fair to you," I said. "I can't—"

"Nothing is fair, Avery," Anastasia pulled away and took my chin in her hand. She made me look at her in the eyes, "If you chose me, not only it wouldn't be fair to Alex, but also to yourself."

I stared into her golden eyes speechless.

"May I kiss your lips for one last time?" she said, smiling sadly.

Tears threatened to roll off my eyes, but I nodded before I could break down and cry again. Anastasia tightened her hold around me. Then she leaned in to press her soft beautiful lips on mine. Tears streamed down my cheeks as I realized it was, in fact, our goodbye kiss.

We parted from each other again. Ana brushed the tears from my face with her thumb and tugged a strand of hair behind my ear.

"Thank you for these wonderful memories," she said with a genuine smile. I smiled back as best as I could. Then she took my hand and we started walking back into the house together.

But when we got inside the hall, Victor appeared with a wary look on his pale face.

"My lady!" he said, sounding as if the house was on fire.

Anastasia released me and turned to look at the man. It seemed like Ana could almost smell a bad omen in the air. I knew something was seriously wrong.

"What's wrong?" she asked.

"This arrived last morning from Moscow," he said and handed an envelope to Anastasia. She opened it and took a creamy white letter out.

I looked at the piece of paper then at Anastasia's face, wishing I could decipher something through her expression. I had a feeling that something wasn't right. And the dreadful part came when Ana's eyes widened in obvious alarm. Her face turned paler as she looked back at me. Her hand trembled trying to grip onto the letter as if it contained a message too heavy.

"What's that, Anastasia?" I asked, already fearing the answer.

"Avery, it's..." she struggled with words and gulped dryly before she spoke again, "...it's Alex."

"What, what's with Alex?" I asked again, a panic chill running inside my stomach. "Ana, just tell me!"

Anastasia took a deep shaky breath before she continued.

"There was an assassination in Moscow, and now Alex is..." she began in a trembling voice.

Before she could finish, I felt as if the light got sucked out of the world. And not until Anastasia caught me in her arms that I realized I was swaying to the side from the weightlessness. Sorrow and shock rolled into one. My chest felt so hollow and heavy at the same time. I almost threw up from all this enormous pain that I couldn't digest.

"No!" was all I could hear myself screaming. "No! No! This can't be!"

I pushed Anastasia's hands away and started to run out of the hall. My feet seemed to have a life of their own. I felt like I could've run all the way to Russia if Anastasia hadn't stopped me.

"Avery wait!" Anastasia pulled me back by the waist, "Avery, just calm down!"

"It's my fault!" I sobbed violently. "It should be me! Not Alex! No!"

"She's not dead!" Ana hissed. "And it's not your fault!"

That stopped my hysteric cries. I turned to Ana again.

"But...but you said..."

"The letter said she was in dire condition. She's not dead," she clarified. I snatched the letter from her hand with a little hint of hope, but it was all written in Russian.

"But Avery...Alex's dying, isn't she?" Anastasia said again. "I have to go back to Kremlin to see her or..." but she trailed off.

"Oh my god," I threw my hands over my mouth, trying not to breath in the grief-stricken air once again. "Anastasia, you have to let me go with you."

"No, Avery, now Moscow's a dangerous place, the hunters..."

"I don't care!" I yelled. "I have to go! Oh god, please, Anastasia, I have to go back to Alex. She needs me, and...and...I need her."

I burst out crying in Ana's arms again. After a long suffering silence later, Anastasia bit her lips and then she nodded.

"Alright, we will go together."

CHAPTER 45

I had never been so terrified in my life that every breath I took agonized me. The constant craving for the person I longed for and how I might not be able to satisfy its hunger. And now my personal torment was still a never-ending course.

"Ana," I whispered to Anastasia, who sat near me in the car after we got off the plane.

"Yes?" she said, turning her face to me.

"Who did that to Alex?"

"You don't want to hear about it now,"

"I've heard from Victor, that someone betrayed her, is that true?" I said. Ana looked at me for a moment and then she nodded.

"Who's the traitor?"

Anastasia was silent.

"Who?" I asked again.

"Nikol," she finally said with a sigh.

Even I had an inkling that someone close to Alex did that, but I could never have guessed it was her. Her hatred toward me had gone too deep, it cost Alex's life.

As if Anastasia could read my mind, she took my hand in hers.

"Avery, trust me, it's not you," she said then stroked my tear-stained cheek with her thumb. "You're not the reason why Nikol did that to Alex. Don't blame yourself."

"No," I said. "This wouldn't have happened if I was sold to someone else if we all had never met."

"Avery, how could you say that?" Anastasia took my face in her palms, forcing me to look at her in the eyes. "You are the best thing that has ever happened to us. You don't know how much Alex has changed because of you. For years, she'd been imprisoned in her own darkness and painful past. But then you came along, and just as you did to me, you freed her."

"But now Alex is dying!" I said, dropping my head in my hands and cried again. "I'm not going to live another day without her. I just can't."

"Avery," Anastasia wrapped her arms around my shoulders, "We still have hope. I can save her."

"She was stabbed through the heart, Ana!" I cried in frustration. "You told me yourself that anything could die! How could we save her?"

"My blood," she said. "I told you that we're quite different from the rest."

"What if it doesn't work?"

"It has to be," she said. "I will do everything in my power to bring Alex back to you."

Even so, I could hear the uncertainty in her voice. I knew we were hopelessly hoping that somehow the miracles would happen.

At last, we arrived at the palace ground, but we were not in Kremlin. The plane had landed at the airbase of St. Petersburg. It was where the state residence of the Russian emperors once located. I recognized the building complex immediately.

The famous Hermitage, the Menshikov Palace, and the Winter Palace soon came into view. I had only seen this beautiful place from some art galleries.

Now here I was, with a heart felt like lead.

The parade of royal cars shot through the main gate in full-speed even we were already inside the palace square. Yet nothing was fast enough for my feverish heart. The anticipation to see Alex kept gnawing at me. Once the cars stopped, everyone flew out of the seats.

Royal guards spread around the doors of the palace. We were not far away from Catherine Palace and the Menshikov. Victor also came with us.

"Your highness, our source has been investigating another lead of this assassination," he said. "Besides Nikol and the hunters' plotting the attack, there was still another person behind it."

"I already know who that is," Anastasia said, her jaw clenched as she spoke the name, "Grigori Rasputin."

There were guards at every entrance as they lead us inside. The building had huge marble columns with classic sculptures and Renaissance paintings. After a long walk through many hallways, we got into the elevator and instead of going up, we went downward.

The elevator doors slid open. I realized there was another version of the building underground.

"This way, your highness," a royal guard ushered us through the hall. As we were getting closer, my aching heartbeats and worried thoughts also grew louder. We reached the end of another long corridor. The guards pushed open a giant steel door, revealing a massive room. It was so big and so cold.

We walked further inside. Our feet echoed on the icy marble floor. A burning fireplace was set in the center of the place, but its warmth wasn't enough to ease the chill. I felt my body shivering. Then we saw a group of men in long black coats standing beside an enormous glowing glass bed. Misty vapors floated around the area. And a silhouette of someone lying there just turned my blood into ice. A long red silk robe with embroidered gold reeds covered the delicate frame.

"Oh my god, Alex!" I ran up toward her. She still looked the same, as if she was just sleeping. But at the same time, she looked as if she could sleep for thousands of years, or even forever. I came to her bedside and placed my hand on her soft cold cheek. "Alex, please, wake up. I'm here."

Hot tears stung my eyes. Anastasia pulled me gently from her sister.

"Let me through, Avery," she said. "I need to check on her."

I backed away and watched Ana biting her own wrist like she did before. Thick red blood flowed out. Anastasia lifted Alex's head from the bed and placed her bleeding hand to her mouth.

"Come on, drink it, Alex. You have to survive this," Ana said in a desperate tone. I clutched my hands to my chest. I was praying for whatever force out there in the universe to save her.

After a while, Anastasia pulled her hand away and came to check on Alex's chest. A line of raw wound started to patch up and heal back to normal. But instead of looking relieved, Ana had a deep questioning frown on her face.

"What's wrong?" I asked, but she turned back to me with tears glistened in her eyes. She shook her head in despair. I let out a howl of anguish as I understood.

"No!" I threw myself over Alex's body again. "You can't leave me like that!"

"She's gone, Avery."

"No! NO!"

"Your highness," a man who I didn't recognize came up and spoke for the first time. "The heart is a natural engine that runs on its own. No amount of blood could revive it if it has lost all its essence and purpose."

I didn't understand what that meant, but the next thing I knew, Anastasia flashed forward and pinned the man against one of the marble columns. Everyone in the room froze.

"You think I don't know what you did to my sister, Rasputin?" she hissed in pure rage, her eyes glowed like burning charcoal. "We trusted you!"

"My dear Anastasiya, you can kill me anytime you wish," Rasputin said calmly though his voice was tight and faint. "I won't deny the consequence of my own action. But your sister needs more than just the essence of your rich royal blood to wake her up again."

"Shut up, you traitor!" Ana threw the man across the hall. His back slammed against the wall and collapsed to the floor again. Blood spurted from his mouth. Several royal guards came to seize Rasputin, holding him down on his knees.

"Get him out of my face and lock him up until I decide when he must die," Anastasia said and the guards moved the man away.

I had never seen Anastasia being like that. But I was too paralyzed to care. Nothing mattered anymore. Turning back to Alex, I reached my hand out and caressed her face. Her soft skin was ice cold against my touch. Alex was still lost in another realm too far away; I couldn't imagine the distance between us. Then I leaned down to kiss her forehead gently. A droplet of my own tear fell onto her cheek. I wiped it away as I kept staring with longing at my lover.

Tracing my hand over her silent chest, I tried to feel the heart that had lost all its essence and purpose.

All of a sudden, something about Rasputin's words clicked in my brain. A new birth of overwhelming hope surged through my bones.

I rose from the bed and made my way toward Victor.

"Victor, I need your help," I said as I gripped the collar of his shirt like a crazy person. "No matter what happens, you have to keep Anastasia away from me and Alex. You hear me?"

He stared at me with a blank look, unable to grasp my intention.

"Avery!" Ana came to pry my hands off the man. "What are you doing?"

"You know why Alex won't wake up?" I turned around to look at her. "It's because she thinks she has lost me! She thinks there is nothing worth living for," I said, hot tears running down my cheeks. "Alex loves me so much that her life depends on my essence, Anastasia, just as mine depends on hers! If she dies, then so will I."

"No!" Ana yelled. "I've already given my blood, but nothing worked!"

"It's not your blood her heart craves. It's mine!" I said. "Please Anastasia, let me try it."

"You don't know what you're dealing with, Avery," she shook my shoulders. "Even if it works, Alex won't be conscious enough to stop herself. The predatory instinct, the bloodlust of a vampire, and the fresh out of death hunger, they will all kick in. I know what it was like the last time we woke up a hundred years ago. If Alex can't get enough of your blood, she will die instantly and so will you. It's a lost cause, Avery. Either one of you dies or both! I can't lose you too!"

"I will take my chances," I said as calmly as I could and turned to Victor again. "Now you decide."

"Victor!"

"Anastasia, you promised me!" I snapped at her. "You said you would do everything to bring Alex back!"

"But that's not how it should be!" she said.

I looked at Victor, willing him to take action.

"It's Alexandra Romanov, Victor, Grand Duchess of Russia. I'm just a human slave," I said in a slow clear voice, letting the words sink into his head. The man flinched as he considered it for a moment and then with a shaky hand, he motioned to the guards.

"Don't you dare, Victor!" Anastasia hissed.

"My apology, your highness," he said before ordered his men. "The girl has made her choice."

"No!"

After that, all I saw was body parts flying like a whirlwind. Crashing sounds echoed off the ceiling. As Anastasia fought back, several royal guards got knocked off then and again. Of course, she was stronger than any of them, but more and more soldiers came in. They each grasped a hold of the young princess, pulling her with great effort toward the steel door. Finally, Ana was pushed away by a wave of black-coated soldiers.

"Avery, no!"

The heavy door started to shut. Before the other guards began bracing it, I caught a glimpse of my former love and mouthed a final farewell.

"Goodbye, Anastasia."

Then I turned around and got onto the bed with Alex.

Staring at those closed eyes with my throat tightened. I leaned in and engraved a kiss on her lips.

Looking at her divine face one more time, I lifted her lifeless body up into a seated position. One of my hands wound around her body as I unbuttoned my shirt with the other, baring enough of my shoulders. Then I took a hairpin from my lock and gave a sharp slash on my exposed skin, letting a line of fresh blood formed.

I could still hear the banging and screaming outside the door as Anastasia tried to break through it. I could hear her desperate calls of my name. It filled with misery and heartbreak. Victor winced and walked away. I pulled Alex into my embrace and placed her soft cold lips against my bleeding cut.

"Alex," I whispered into her ear. "Come back to me, please."

I clung onto her tightly, willing her to drink from my blood as if it was the only way our souls could merge and become one. But her unresponsive lips still rested on my shoulder. Not a slight lap of the tongue was taken place.

"No Alex, don't do this to me," I said as desperate tears welled up even more.

For a moment, I didn't know what to do. My mind went overdrive. Millions of thoughts flashed back and forth. Memories of us together in the past few months jumbled inside my head. They kept rushing in until I lost my grip on reality. And just like that, I was transported back to the time where Alex and I were together.

"Will you be my rose princess?"

Her golden voice resonated like blissful music in my ears. The heart-warming memory made me smile in spite of myself. I said the only thing I longed to say for the first time.

"I love you."

Suddenly, I felt light-headed as if I had just channeled the most powerful energy out of every cell in my body. Then a slight tickle on my skin broke my train of thoughts. The tingling feeling rushed through my core as a new realization of Alex weakly nibbling on my skin.

"Oh my god," was all I could utter. This time, tears of worldly joy liberated themselves from my eyes. The taste of my blood awoke her senses. I could feel the tiny tips of her fangs finding their way into my willing flesh. Their sharp edges poked through the soft tissue of my skin as my love was becoming alive again.

Everything started like a miracle. Alex was growing stronger as she kept feeding on the blood from my veins. Her soft velvety tongue lapped over my skin. How I longed for this wonderful touch. By now, I no longer felt the throbbing pain. It was nothing but bittersweet joy.

Until the chill seeped into my body, I realized I was being pulled into the realm of nothingness myself. I tried not to let go of Alex, but my hands and eyelids felt too heavy. No matter how hard I fought to stay awake, the last light inside me slowly began to fade.

CHAPTER 46

ALEXANDRA

I was drifting beyond this physical world of time and space. Until all my senses were wide awake, like the first blossom of spring. Like a spark of music to wake me from this endless dream. One touch at a time formed a sensation. A burst of electrifying jolts brought back fragments of my thoughts one by one. My hands wrapped around a small frame of someone. I felt like a newborn, suckling with hunger and wants.

Ravenous growls echoed from the depth of my stomach. Sinking my teeth deeper, I wanted to get more of this blissful liquid taste. It was like sweet nectar or rich ambrosia to my thirsty mouth.

For some reason, everything felt wrong to me. Something about a glowing effect that I couldn't see yet it was there, like a candle that wipes out darkness. It was stronger than the craving.

I could smell the familiar scent that floated in and out my nostrils. The wonderful taste I knew all too well was blood itself. But there was something about the pressure against my skin, and the soothing warmth that radiated into my body. I could have ignored everything and let my monstrous side took over. But my heart was pounding in a frantic tempo as if it was trying to find another rhythm that matches its own.

For the first time, I made a conscious effort to open my eyes. Once I succeeded, it felt as though I was swimming in the sea of dizziness and buzzing sounds. The world seemed askew to me.

I found my hands entangled with the soft silky hair that I felt familiar with. They were still roaming over the smooth flawless skin longingly. I was drinking from someone's blood, and not just anyone. Even without looking, I could feel how important this person was to me. The one and only person my heart ached for.

Then the sight of bright crimson blood appeared to my hazy eyes. I began to panic. With my newly recovered strength, I unclenched my jaw, ignoring the sweet delicious smell. At last, I was able to pull the sharp long canines back inside and unhooked my mouth from the desirable taste.

I looked around myself, noticing the fresh blood dripped down my chin. Then I was faced with the most unimaginable moment in my life. Avery's pale beautiful face was inches away from mine. Her skin was almost icy cold against my body. It was obviously from the loss of too much blood. I gasped, dropping my blood-stained jaw, losing my voice to shock. Tears burst out from my eyes as I realized the whole time I was drinking from her. Her blood awoke me. No, not only that, her whole presence did. Her essence, her loving soul had found me in the sea of emptiness. But now here I was, holding her empty self in my arms like that of a cruel predator I always was.

I wanted to scream until the world comes crumbling down on me.

CHAPTER 47

ANASTASIA

I punched one of the royal guards hard. He stumbled back and yelped in pain. I kicked the other in the stomach and flipped another off my back to the ground. My hands twisted his hand at the joints until I heard a crack. The poor guard cried on the floor. I was mad with anger and heartache.

By then, no one dared to touch me anymore. Their fear of getting hurt like their fellows was visible on their hard faces.

"Your highness, please forgive us. We're only following the order," they apologized, bowing in surrender.

"Your job is to do as I say!" I yelled. "Now open the freaking door now or I'll rip all your heads off!"

"But Grand Duchess Alexandra..."

"*Now!*" I said, rushing at a blinding speed to one of the royal guards and lifted him off the floor by the throat. My eyes were ablaze with a burning rage. If anything happened to Avery, I wasn't sure I could stop myself from destroying everything in sight. The other guards looked at each other in nervousness but then they decided to move to the steel door.

"Open the door for her highness," they ordered their comrades from the inside.

At last, the entrance went ajar. I pushed them aside and spotted Avery from across the hall. I couldn't feel any more frightened than when I saw Alex holding the girl with her face buried into her neck.

"Alex no!" I shot off like there were rockets fired from my heels. All I knew was I had to stop my sister. Her not being herself after coming back to life was predictable and dangerous. I didn't have the time to feel relieved seeing my sister alive again. Not when Avery was lying on the bed completely still. Her face was too pale for a human. Alex's shoulders seemed to shake, but I couldn't see her face.

I rushed over and grabbed Alex by her shoulders, pulling her away from Avery. She wouldn't budge. Alex was probably in a frenzy feeding that she no longer recognized anyone.

"Alexandra, stop!" I cried and looped my arms around hers before I dragged her away with all my might. She got off Avery at last, but then she turned around and snapped her teeth at me. I blocked her crazy bites, trying to shield her off. Victor came to help me, but Alex swatted him off like a bug. He went flying across the room. Other vampires stood by, too afraid to intervene.

My sister wasn't as strong, but it was obvious she had lost her mind. And madness made her vicious and uncontrollable.

"Alex, it's me!" I yelled. "I'm your sister, Anastasia."

In a split second, a flash of recognition crossed her feverish eyes. Then the madness began to subside as if memories seemed to catch up with her.

But after a moment, Alex's tears rolled off her cheeks. Her face contorted with confusion and regret.

"Av...Avery..." she finally formed her first word. Her face turned into a terrified shade. "I killed Avery."

With those words, my heart stopped. I pushed my sister off of me and went back to the sleeping girl on the bed. Alex also came to Avery's side. Her hands shook visibly as she brought them to her lover's blood-drained face.

"Oh god, what have I done?" Alex kept saying over and over, shaking her head to herself.

"Avery sacrificed herself to bring you back," I said in a whisper. "She let you drink her blood so that you could wake up."

"Oh...stupid girl..." Alex cried then she turned to look at me. "Why didn't you stop her?!"

"I tried!" I said. "But she didn't listen."

"Anastasia..." she swallowed hard as she looked at me. Tears streamed down her cheeks without ceasing. "Anastasia please, you have to turn her for me."

I wanted more than anything to make Avery open her eyes again. But the truth was, the girl's last breath was gone. Her link to this world was completely broken. And worse Alex refused to accept it. I felt like the earth had stopped spinning.

"Alex...she's....she's gone. I can't turn her." I shook my head in despair. The venom had stopped her heart. And even if I gave her my vampire blood, there was no guarantee that she would turn.

"No! Avery is not dead! You have to try! She's my life. I can't lose her. Oh, Anastasia, please!" Alex begged me through her tears. "If you don't change her, I will!"

"You're not strong enough to do it, Alex," I said. "You might as well kill yourself!"

"I don't care! It's better than living without her," she sobbed.

I had never seen my older sister cried so much, not even when we saw our family being murdered.

I bit my lips, and with the deepest, most horrible pain of losing the girl I had loved, I had to go against the truth. They say miracles won't happen twice, but I prayed against all odd, that this time was an exception.

I brought my wrist to my mouth and slit it with my sharp teeth. Blood gushed out once again, dripping furiously onto the bed. I lifted Avery's head from the bed and put my bleeding hand to her mouth. Trying to get as much as blood into her system was almost impossible. I had to make her swallow. I withdrew my hand back. Alex frowned at the interruption. I ignored her and sucked my own blood from my wrist before feeding Avery mouth-to-mouth. Her lips were as cold as ice against my own. This once lively skin was unresponsive against mine. All the while, my sister was watching with a desperate look on her face. I didn't stop until my blood spilled back up as a sign Avery could take no more.

I pulled myself away, breathing harder than ever.

"Avery, my dear love, please wake up. I need you here with me," Alex cooed at her lifeless lover as she stroked her cheek. "You know how much I love you, please, don't kill me this way."

My sister picked up the love of her life, her whole essence and eternity. She held her against her sobbing chest, rocking back and forth as she whispered pleadingly in her ear. My feet felt wobbly as I tried to stand up and stepped back from the devastating sight. I couldn't find anything more heartbreaking than the tragedy of a lover. And then my knees buckled. I collapsed to the floor and the whole world spun around me.

As I stared up into the void of loss and grief, I knew this was over.

CHAPTER 48

As I sat inside an open-air gazebo, I watched the salty gentle breeze blew over the palm trees. Above the clear aqua-blue water, I watched herons filled up the tropical plants. Others went soaring in the high blue sky, going out of their nests for the morning hunt. Little birds chirped away over the blinding white beach.

I breathed in the fresh humid air of serenity and tried to soak up the new reality I was thrown into. Then a musical voice drifted through the gentle wind. A new rush of vibrating zeal burst through my veins. I knew that sweet delicate tone. My face lighted up into a smile, already anticipating the presence of my other half.

"Alex!"

I stood up and turned around to find a stunning girl in her beautiful pink pastel dress. It flowed and rippled over her elegant frame down to her knees. She pushed the sunglasses up her straight nose and adjusted her straw hat on her wind-blown hair.

"You're up too early," Avery said as she ran up into the gazebo towards me. I opened my arms and welcomed her onto my embrace. Avery hurled herself at me, and I stumbled back. She just forgot her newfound strength again. We collapsed onto a loveseat together, buried ourselves in the soft pillows. She giggled and took off her straw hat, letting her dark brown hair flow over her slender shoulders. I took her sunglasses off and gazed into her bright violet eyes. They sparkled and danced like precious gems.

The thought of Avery being a newborn hadn't crossed my mind until I witnessed her human qualities slowly magnified. Her natural beauty became so enchanting to the point it took my breath away every time I looked at her. Though I always thought she was beautiful as a human, I had never seen her more graceful and lively like she was now. She wrapped her arms around my neck and gazed at me with a smile plastered on her alluring lips. I looked back at that doll-like face of my lover.

For a moment I found myself unable to speak. I was speechless from all the contentment that life bestowed on me. I thought this only existed in fantasies, but now reality was better than my dream.

I had decided that my whole existence would come to an end when I thought I had lost Avery forever. But the fate always has a way with irony. Then again, I would never trade for anything else in the world. Avery was worth all my pains, my tears, and most importantly she was worth my love.

"Good morning princess," I said. Avery cocked her head as she hovered over me.

"Shouldn't I be the one to say that to you?" she said.

"In my heart, you're the real princess," I said. "The princess I've been dreaming of ever since I was a little girl."

"You and your honeyed words."

"Don't hold back if you want to taste them on my lips," I said. She tipped my nose playfully with her index finger.

"Who said I want to?" she pretended to scoff back. I giggled. Unable to curb my affection for her anymore, I started trailing kisses over her neck. Avery squirmed away with a shy yelp.

"Aw Alex, stop!"

"I can't, my love," I said, tightened my arms around her waist to keep her from moving. "I want to make sure that you are real and not my own imagination."

"It's already been months and you still couldn't get used to it?" she teased me back. "I think you're slower than usual ever since you woke up."

"Well, I just think it's better now that I can have sex with you every day of the month," I said with a smirk. Avery's mouth flung open. She slapped my arm.

"You're such a pervert!"

"Ouch," I said and then started tickling her. Avery screamed and laughed in my arms, begging me to stop. When I finally stopped, I kissed her on the corner of her lips. Avery smiled and took my face in her hands and kissed me back on my forehead. I wanted more, but she pulled away and sat up again. Avery still had that beautiful blush. This one thing never changed.

I put my arms around her and lifted her legs up, pulling her onto my lap. We sat looking at the blue sea before us, listening to the waves crashing the white shore. The memory back in Russia seemed like a distant star, burning so far away, yet at the same time, it was always there.

I remember how it almost killed me with all the pain and grief she put me through. If it wasn't for Anastasia, I wouldn't have been here with my Avery. Speaking of Anastasia, I had no idea how she coped with everything. I hadn't seen her since Avery was back. But I still owed my sister this for the rest of my immortality.

It did take Avery longer than usual to turn. Yet she completed the transition at last. I remembered how bright her eyes were once she woke up. It didn't take long for her to recognize me. Of course, there are consequences that come along when you cheat death. But Avery accepted everything with bravery and calmness. It was as if her humanity was still her strongest forte. It was still a shield that protected her from the harsh reality. Her compassion prevented her from giving in to the inner demon of our kind. And I couldn't be any prouder.

"What are you thinking about, Alex?" Avery whispered, noticing my distant expression.

"I'm just so thankful that you came back, Avery."

"Likewise." She smiled, stroking my face. "I'm so very happy to have you."

"Aren't you afraid of what you are now?" I said, brushing her wind-blown hair from her face. As I could tell, she was still having a hard time dealing with the craving for blood. She still had the temptation we all shared, but again, Avery refused to drink from humans at all cost. I guess Anastasia was a big influence on this part. No matter what, my sister still had a place in her heart.

I stared at Avery's twinkling violet eyes. Her impossibly long black lashes shaded them from the rising sun. Then she looked up at me again.

"With you, it's different," she said. "No one makes me feel so safe like you do, Alex."

A smile stitched across my face. I kept staring at her until she blushed again. But her eyes shone brighter, and she looked so content in my arms. I knew it was time. I pulled out a golden box from my pocket. I'd been waiting for this moment a very long time and that made me a bit nervous. My hand shook a little as I held the tiny box to her.

"Give me your hand," I said. Avery's angelic face turned to me and then at the object. Then her blank expression vanished, replaced by the new realization.

She gasped.

"Oh, Alex!" Avery cried, looking astonished. I opened the gold box, revealing a shiny diamond ring. It flicked brightly like rays of rainbow against the light.

"It's so beautiful," Avery whispered.

"That's my mother's wedding ring," I told her. "Now it's yours."

"Oh my god, Alex!" she breathed as joyful tears welled up in her eyes. I took her hand in mine and slipped the ring on her tiny delicate finger. It fit so perfectly. Then I put her palm against my chest as we stared at each other.

"*Vot moe serce. Ono polno lubvi*, here is my heart, and it's full of love."

Avery smiled with pure happiness and then she leaned forward to place her soft lips on mine. And the kiss was like no others before. It was divine, nothing to do with lust or sexual means. It was only the innocent craving of two bonding souls. A kiss that had overcome the darkest of the deep empty space. It was like falling stars in the night sky, a burning flame, and frosting ice. Like pure spring water from the mountain dew. This is what you dream a kiss to be. We would have a kiss just like this every day, forever and always.

ABOUT THE AUTHOR

Svetlana Ivanova first started writing as a hobby. She likes to think of herself as a writer version of a mad scientist, who enjoys creating worlds and lets people's suppressed sexuality and fantasies roam freely. If she isn't writing her stories, she's in class daydreaming about writing her stories.

OTHER BOOKS BY THE AUTHOR:

CURSED BLOOD
BLACK KNIGHT
HADES
STRESSED SPELLED BACKWARDS
DAUGHTER OF THE NAGA
ANASTASIA ROMANOV THE SEQUEL
(COMING SOON)